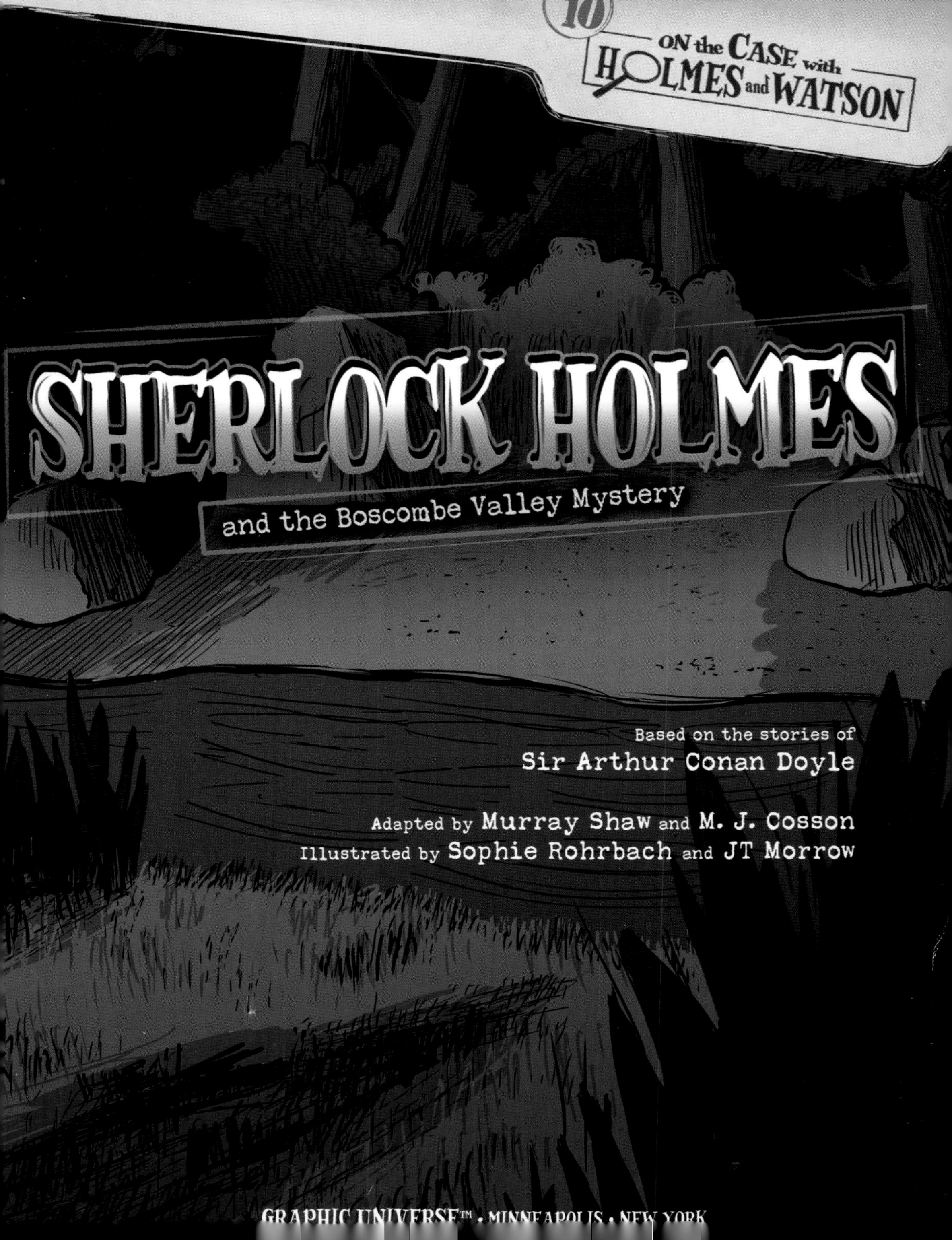

#10 ON the CASE with HOLMES and WATSON

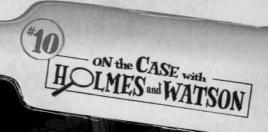

SHERLOCK HOLMES

and the Boscombe Valley Mystery

Based on the stories of
Sir Arthur Conan Doyle

Adapted by Murray Shaw and M. J. Cosson
Illustrated by Sophie Rohrbach and JT Morrow

GRAPHIC UNIVERSE™ • MINNEAPOLIS • NEW YORK

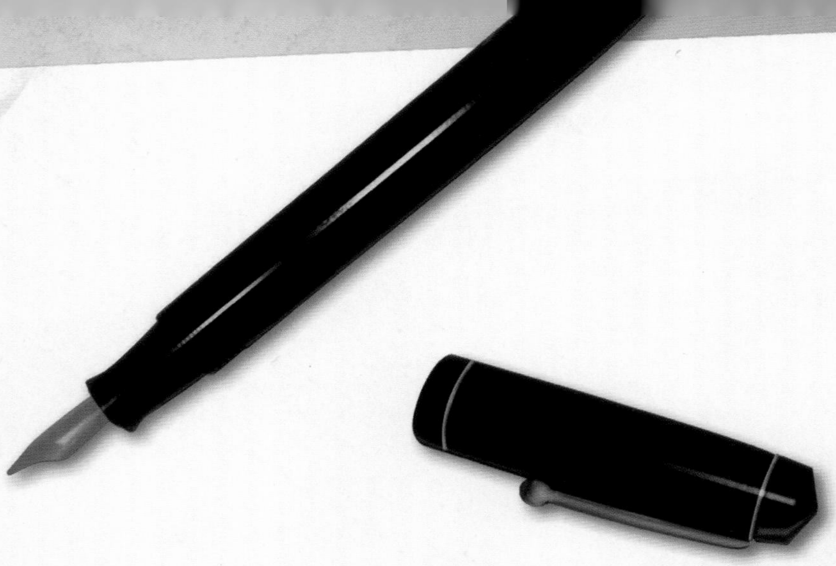

Grateful acknowledgment to Dame Jean Conan Doyle for permission to use the
Sherlock Holmes characters created by Sir Arthur Conan Doyle

Text copyright © 2012 by Murray Shaw
Illustrations © 2012 by Lerner Publishing Group, Inc.

Graphic Universe™ is a trademark of Lerner Publishing Group, Inc.

Graphic Universe™
A division of Lerner Publishing Group, Inc.
241 First Avenue North
Minneapolis, MN 55401 U.S.A.

Website address: www.lernerbooks.com

Library of Congress Cataloging-in-Publication Data

Shaw, Murray.
    Sherlock Holmes and the Boscombe Valley mystery / based on the stories
of Sir Arthur Conan Doyle ; adapted by Murray Shaw and M.J. Cosson ;
illustrated by Sophie Rohrbach and J.T. Morrow.
       p.   cm. — (On the case with Holmes and Watson ; #10)
    Summary: Retold in graphic novel form, Sherlock Holmes attempts
to solve the murder of a Herefordshire landowner, whose estranged son
has been accused of the crime. Includes a section explaining Holmes's
reasoning and the clues he used to solve the mystery.
    ISBN: 978-0-7613-7089-5 (lib. bdg. : alk. paper)
    I. Graphic novels. (I. Graphic novels. 2. Doyle, Arthur Conan, Sir,
1859-1930. Boscombe Valley mystery—Adaptations. 3. Mystery and detective
stories.) I. Cosson, M. J. II. Rohrbach, Sophie, ill. III. Morrow, J. T., ill.
IV. Doyle, Arthur Conan, Sir, 1859-1930. Boscombe Valley mystery. V. Title.
VI. Title: Boscombe Valley mystery.
    PZ7.7.S46Sib 2012   2010040725
    741.5'973—dc22

Manufactured in the United States of America
I—BC—7/15/11

The Story of
SHERLOCK HOLMES
the Famous Detective

Sherlock Holmes and his helpful friend Dr. John Watson are fictional characters created by British writer Sir Arthur Conan Doyle. Doyle published his first novel about the pair, *A Study in Scarlet*, in 1887, and it became very successful. Doyle went on to write fifty-six short stories, as well as three more novels about Holmes's adventures—*The Sign of Four* (1890), *The Hound of the Baskervilles* (1902), and *The Valley of Fear* (1915).

Sherlock Holmes and Dr. Watson have become some of the most famous book characters of all time. Holmes spent most of his time solving mysteries, but he also had a wide array of hobbies, such as playing the violin, boxing, and sword fighting. Watson, a retired army doctor, met Holmes through a mutual friend when Holmes was looking for a roommate. Watson lived with Holmes for several years at 221B Baker Street before marrying and moving out. However, after his marriage, Watson continued to assist Holmes with his cases.

The original versions of the Sherlock Holmes stories are still printed, and many have been made into movies and television shows. Readers continue to be impressed by Holmes's detective methods of observation and scientific reason.

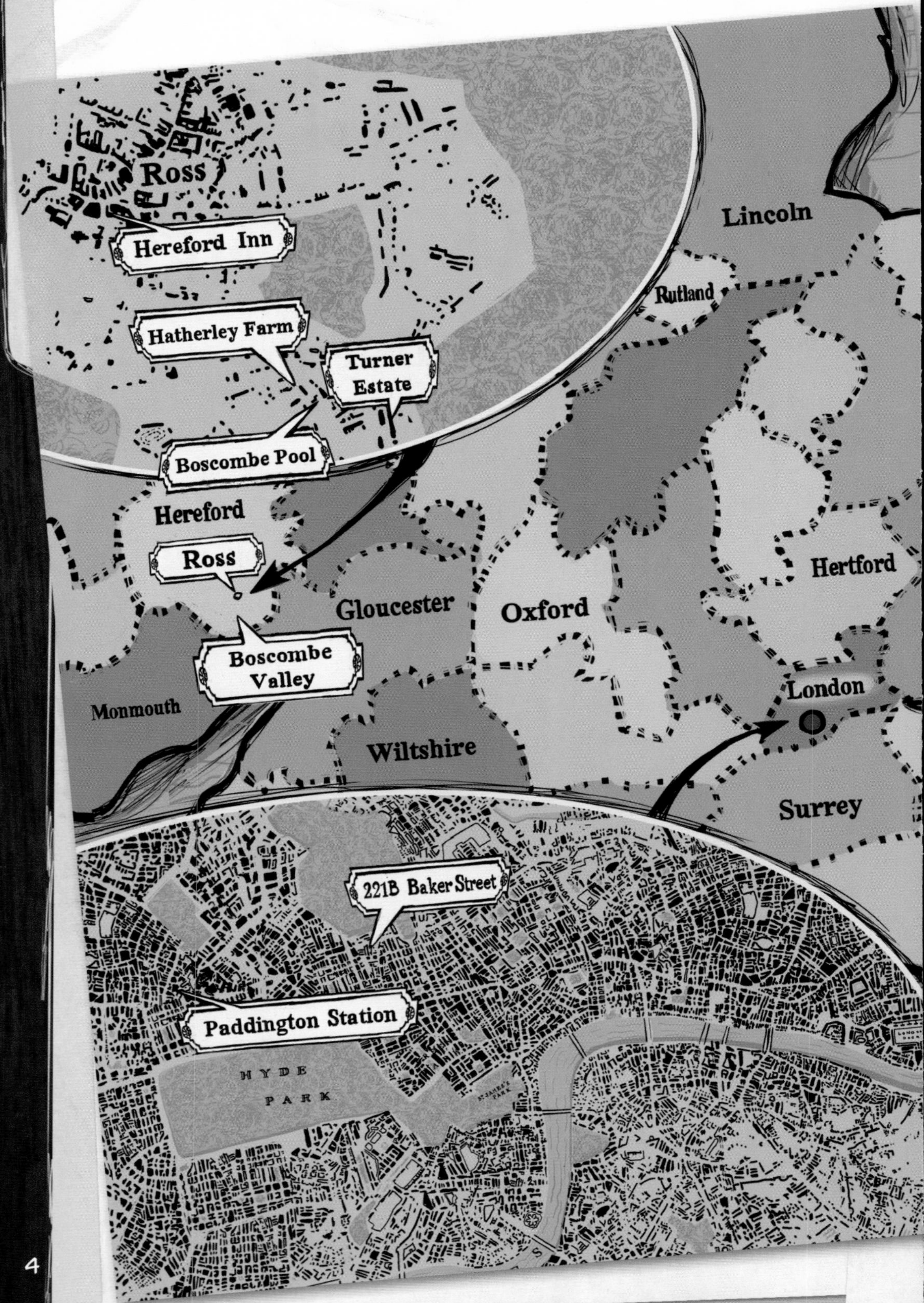
Ross
Hereford Inn
Hatherley Farm
Turner Estate
Boscombe Pool
Lincoln
Rutland
Hereford
Ross
Gloucester
Oxford
Hertford
Boscombe Valley
Monmouth
London
Wiltshire
Surrey
221B Baker Street
Paddington Station
HYDE PARK

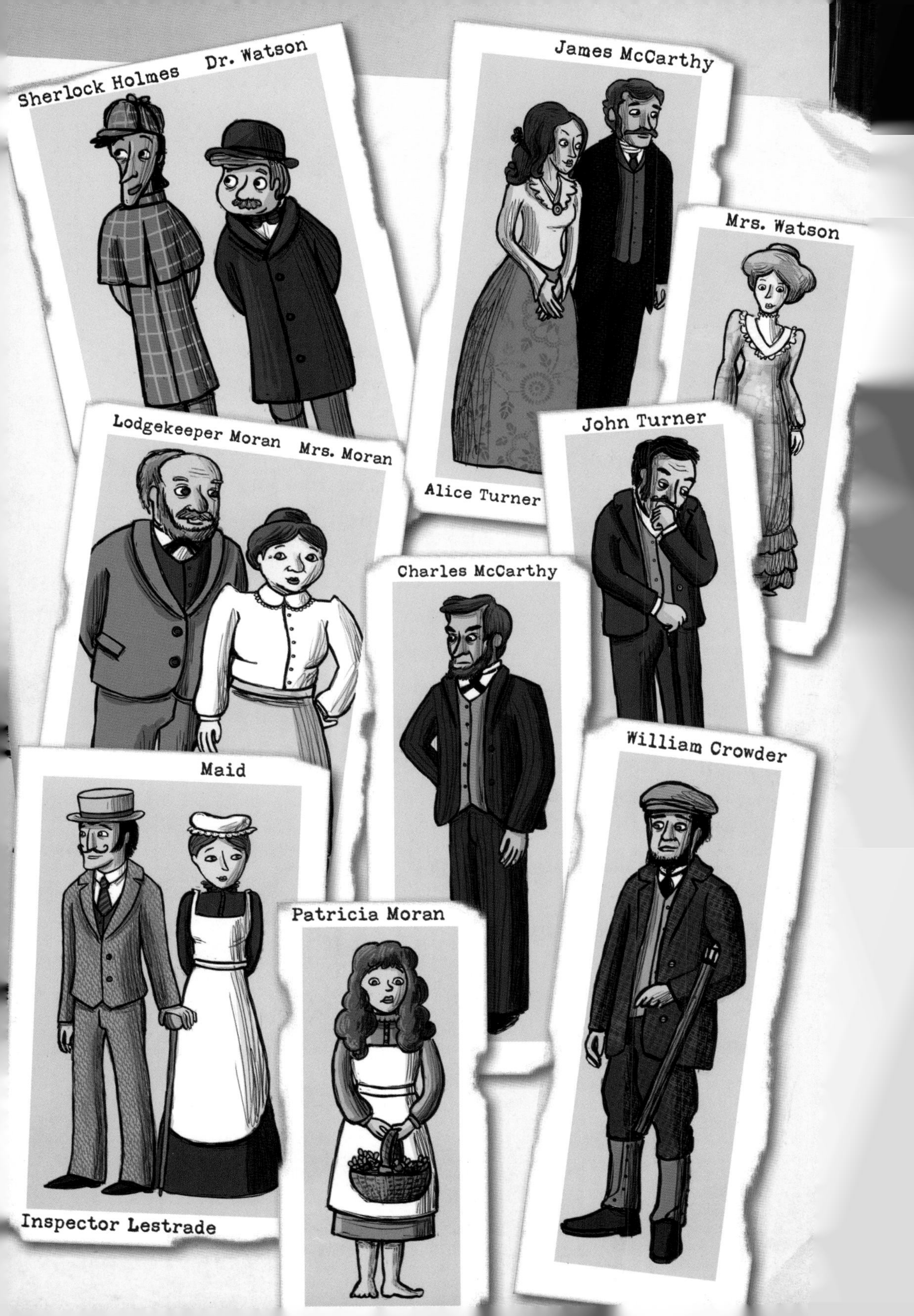
Sherlock Holmes
Dr. Watson
James McCarthy
Alice Turner
Mrs. Watson
Lodgekeeper Moran
Mrs. Moran
John Turner
Charles McCarthy
Maid
Inspector Lestrade
Patricia Moran
William Crowder

From the Desk of
John H. Watson, M.D.

My name is Dr. John H. Watson. For several years, I have been assisting my friend, Sherlock Holmes, in solving mysteries throughout the bustling city of London and beyond. Holmes is a peculiar man—always questioning and reasoning his way through various problems. But when I first met him in 1878, I was immediately intrigued by his oddities.

Holmes has always been more daring than I, and his logical deduction never ceases to amaze me. I have begun writing down all of the adventures I have with Holmes. This is one of those stories.

Sincerely,

Dr. Watson

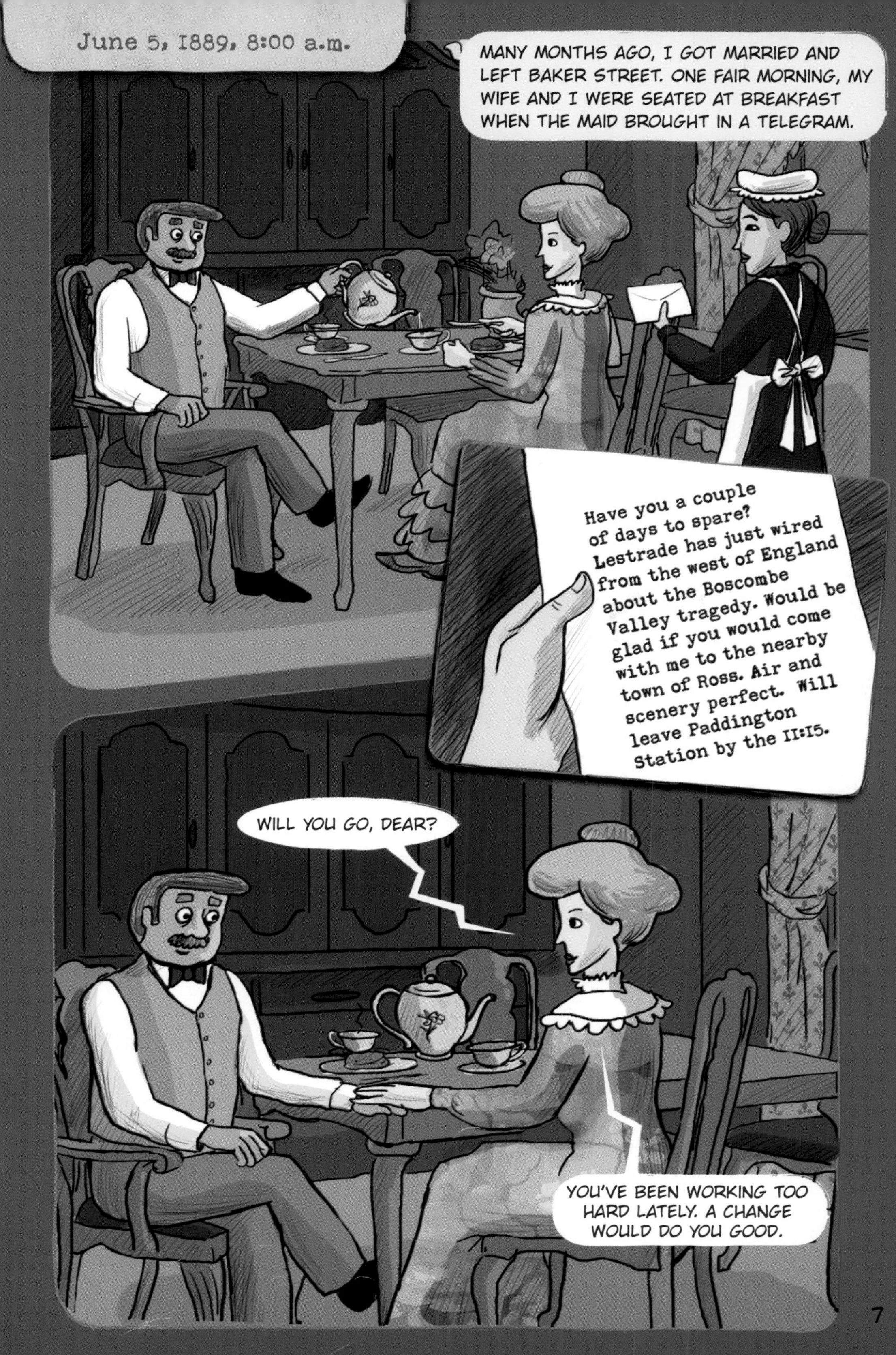
June 5, 1889, 8:00 a.m.
MANY MONTHS AGO, I GOT MARRIED AND LEFT BAKER STREET. ONE FAIR MORNING, MY WIFE AND I WERE SEATED AT BREAKFAST WHEN THE MAID BROUGHT IN A TELEGRAM.
Have you a couple of days to spare? Lestrade has just wired from the west of England about the Boscombe Valley tragedy. Would be glad if you would come with me to the nearby town of Ross. Air and scenery perfect. Will leave Paddington Station by the 11:15.
WILL YOU GO, DEAR?
YOU'VE BEEN WORKING TOO HARD LATELY. A CHANGE WOULD DO YOU GOOD.

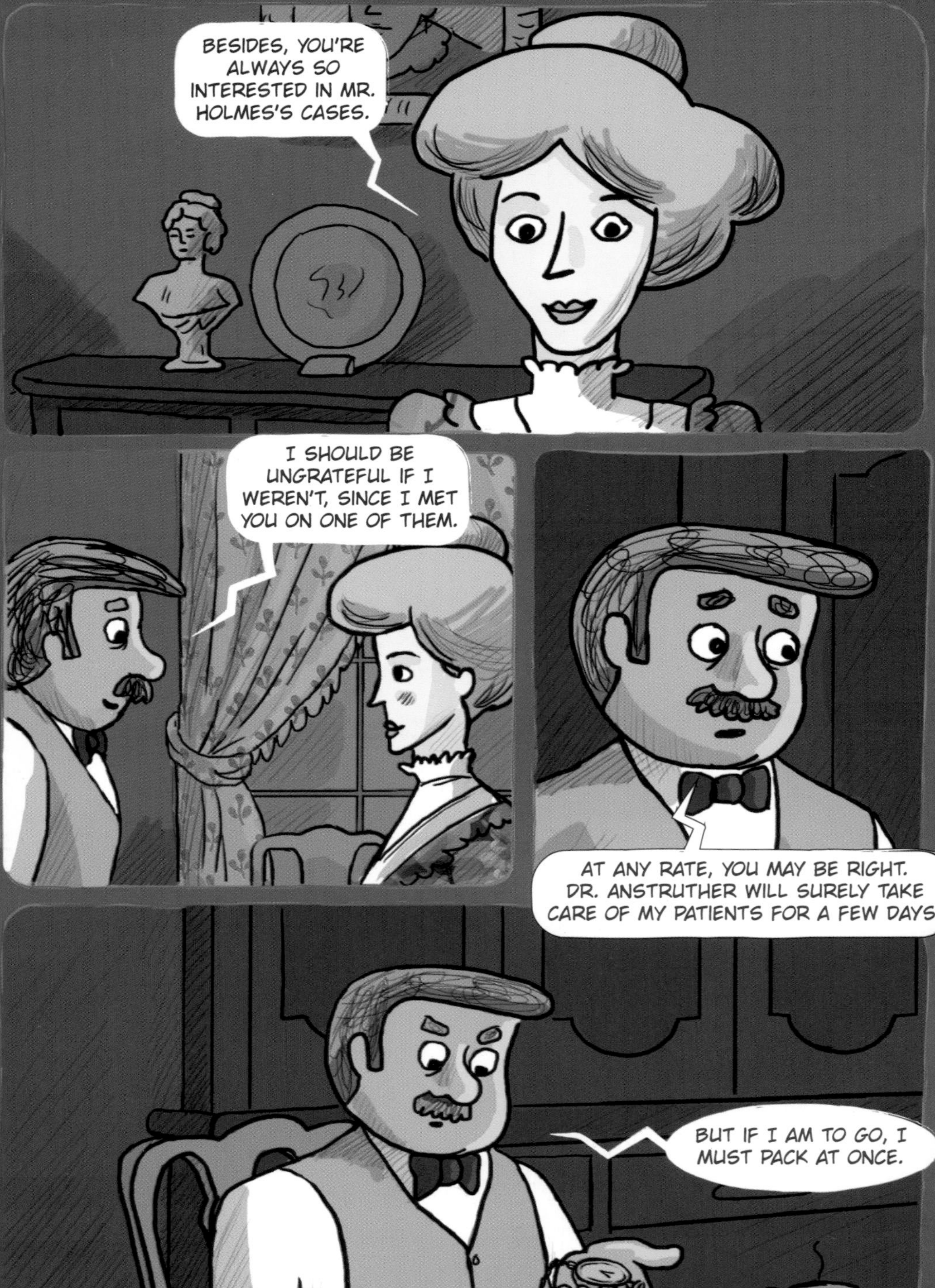

BESIDES, YOU'RE ALWAYS SO INTERESTED IN MR. HOLMES'S CASES.
I SHOULD BE UNGRATEFUL IF I WEREN'T, SINCE I MET YOU ON ONE OF THEM.
AT ANY RATE, YOU MAY BE RIGHT. DR. ANSTRUTHER WILL SURELY TAKE CARE OF MY PATIENTS FOR A FEW DAYS.
BUT IF I AM TO GO, I MUST PACK AT ONCE.

My army experience in Afghanistan had taught me to pack quickly and lightly. So I was soon in a cab, rattling away to Paddington Station. Holmes was awaiting me there, pacing up and down the platform.

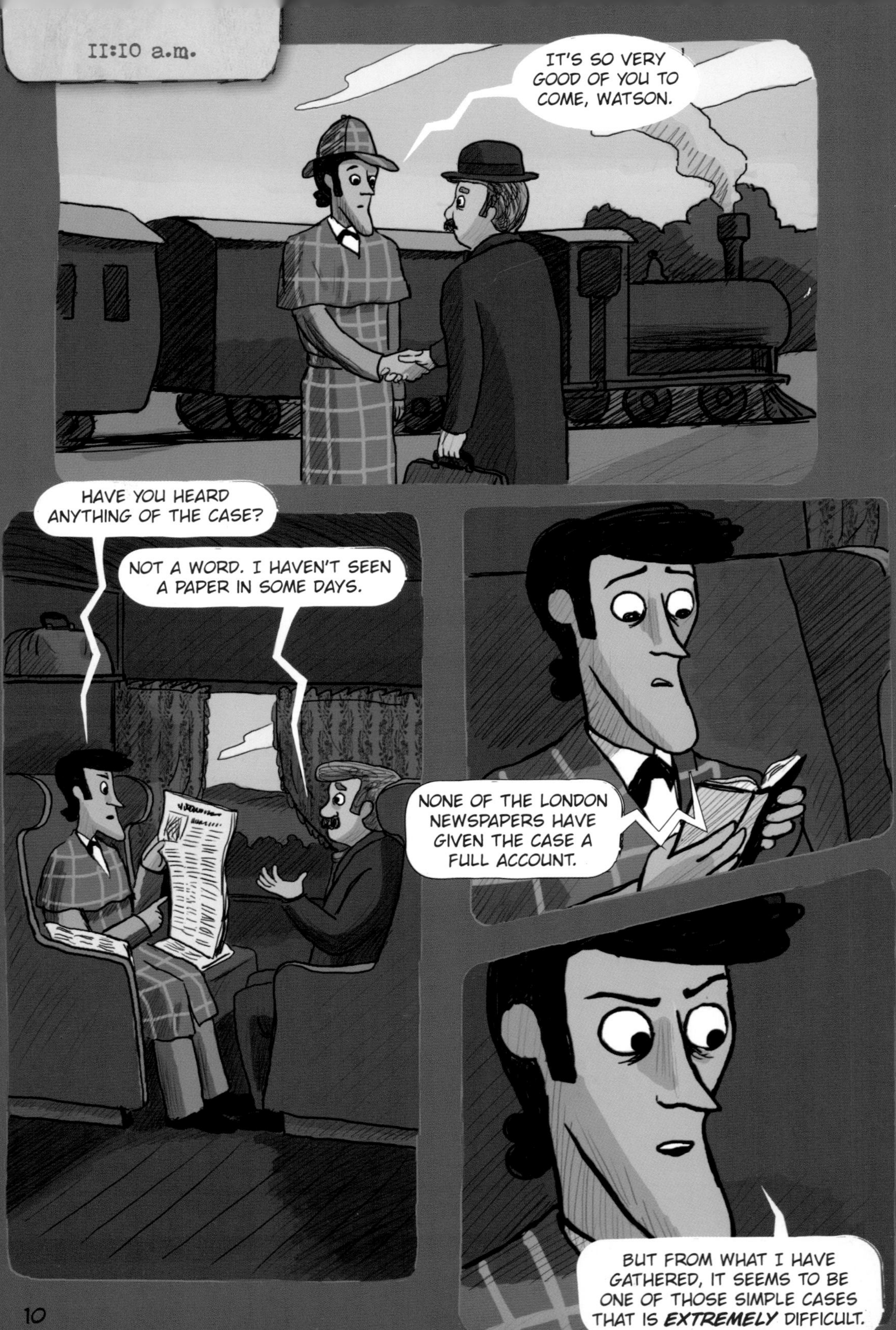

11:10 a.m.
IT'S SO VERY GOOD OF YOU TO COME, WATSON.
HAVE YOU HEARD ANYTHING OF THE CASE?
NOT A WORD. I HAVEN'T SEEN A PAPER IN SOME DAYS.
NONE OF THE LONDON NEWSPAPERS HAVE GIVEN THE CASE A FULL ACCOUNT.
BUT FROM WHAT I HAVE GATHERED, IT SEEMS TO BE ONE OF THOSE SIMPLE CASES THAT IS *EXTREMELY* DIFFICULT.

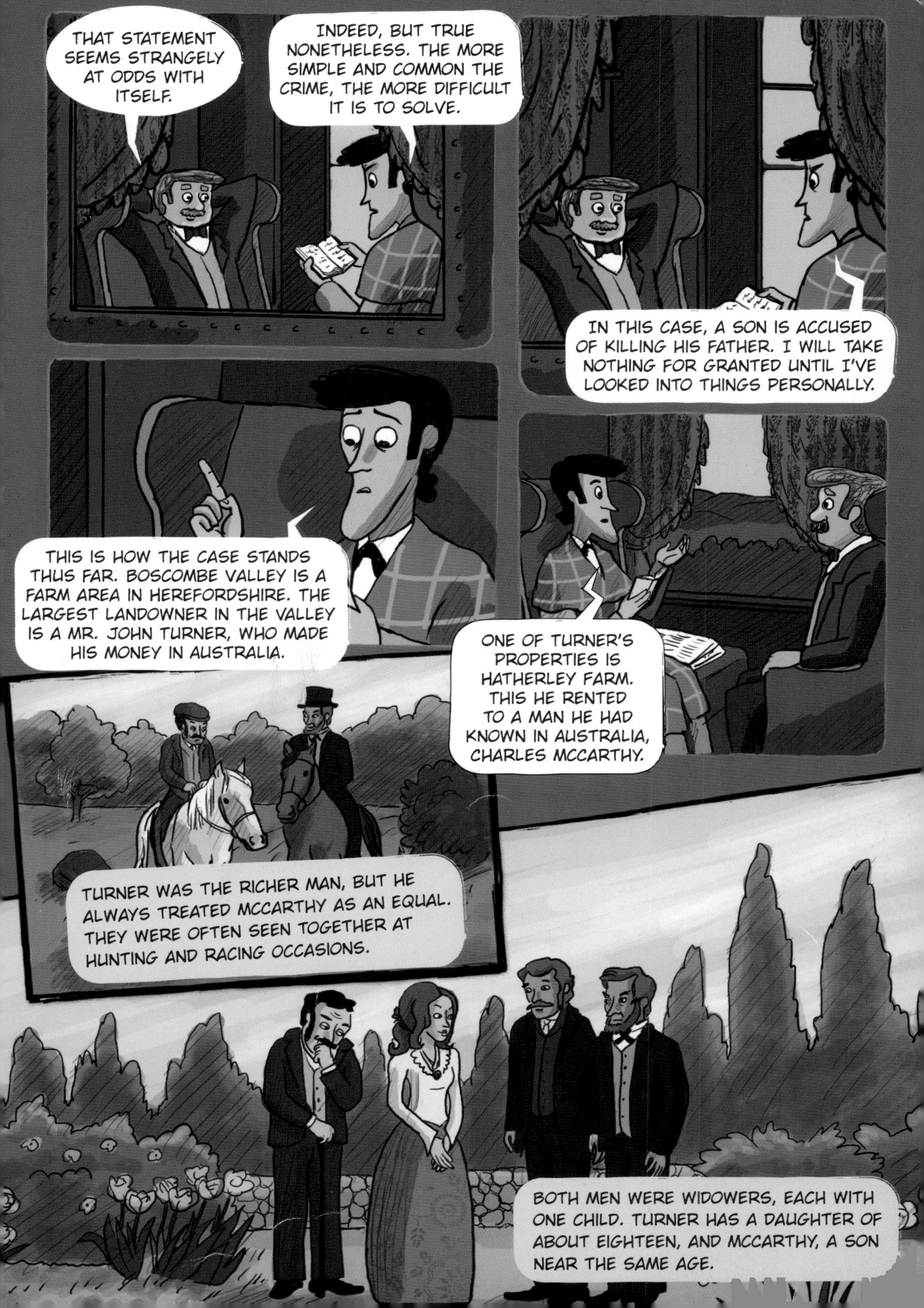
THAT STATEMENT SEEMS STRANGELY AT ODDS WITH ITSELF.
INDEED, BUT TRUE NONETHELESS. THE MORE SIMPLE AND COMMON THE CRIME, THE MORE DIFFICULT IT IS TO SOLVE.
IN THIS CASE, A SON IS ACCUSED OF KILLING HIS FATHER. I WILL TAKE NOTHING FOR GRANTED UNTIL I'VE LOOKED INTO THINGS PERSONALLY.
THIS IS HOW THE CASE STANDS THUS FAR. BOSCOMBE VALLEY IS A FARM AREA IN HEREFORDSHIRE. THE LARGEST LANDOWNER IN THE VALLEY IS A MR. JOHN TURNER, WHO MADE HIS MONEY IN AUSTRALIA.
ONE OF TURNER'S PROPERTIES IS HATHERLEY FARM. THIS HE RENTED TO A MAN HE HAD KNOWN IN AUSTRALIA, CHARLES MCCARTHY.
TURNER WAS THE RICHER MAN, BUT HE ALWAYS TREATED MCCARTHY AS AN EQUAL. THEY WERE OFTEN SEEN TOGETHER AT HUNTING AND RACING OCCASIONS.
BOTH MEN WERE WIDOWERS, EACH WITH ONE CHILD. TURNER HAS A DAUGHTER OF ABOUT EIGHTEEN, AND MCCARTHY, A SON NEAR THE SAME AGE.

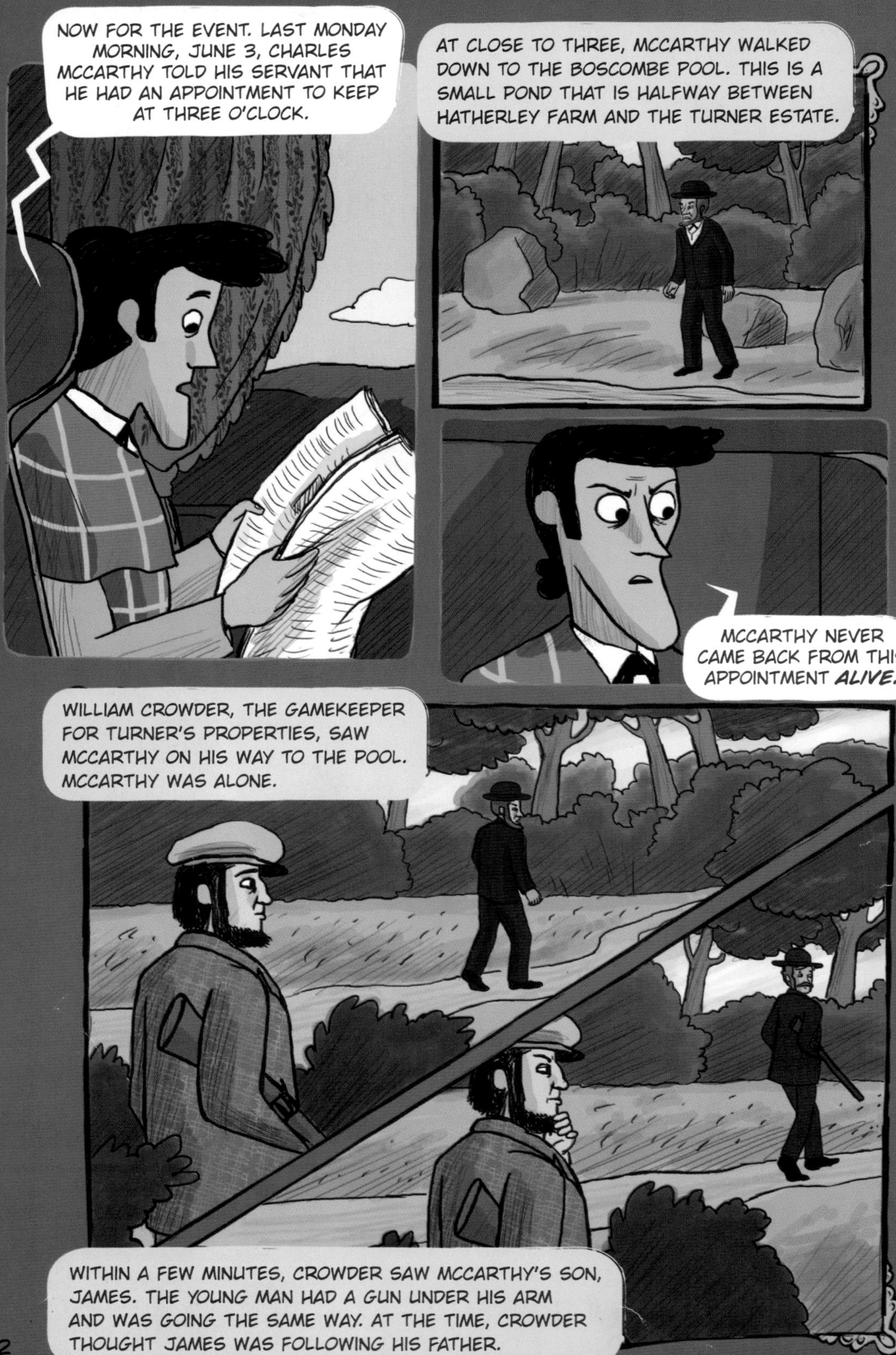
NOW FOR THE EVENT. LAST MONDAY MORNING, JUNE 3, CHARLES MCCARTHY TOLD HIS SERVANT THAT HE HAD AN APPOINTMENT TO KEEP AT THREE O'CLOCK.
AT CLOSE TO THREE, MCCARTHY WALKED DOWN TO THE BOSCOMBE POOL. THIS IS A SMALL POND THAT IS HALFWAY BETWEEN HATHERLEY FARM AND THE TURNER ESTATE.
MCCARTHY NEVER CAME BACK FROM THIS APPOINTMENT ***ALIVE.***
WILLIAM CROWDER, THE GAMEKEEPER FOR TURNER'S PROPERTIES, SAW MCCARTHY ON HIS WAY TO THE POOL. MCCARTHY WAS ALONE.
WITHIN A FEW MINUTES, CROWDER SAW MCCARTHY'S SON, JAMES. THE YOUNG MAN HAD A GUN UNDER HIS ARM AND WAS GOING THE SAME WAY. AT THE TIME, CROWDER THOUGHT JAMES WAS FOLLOWING HIS FATHER.

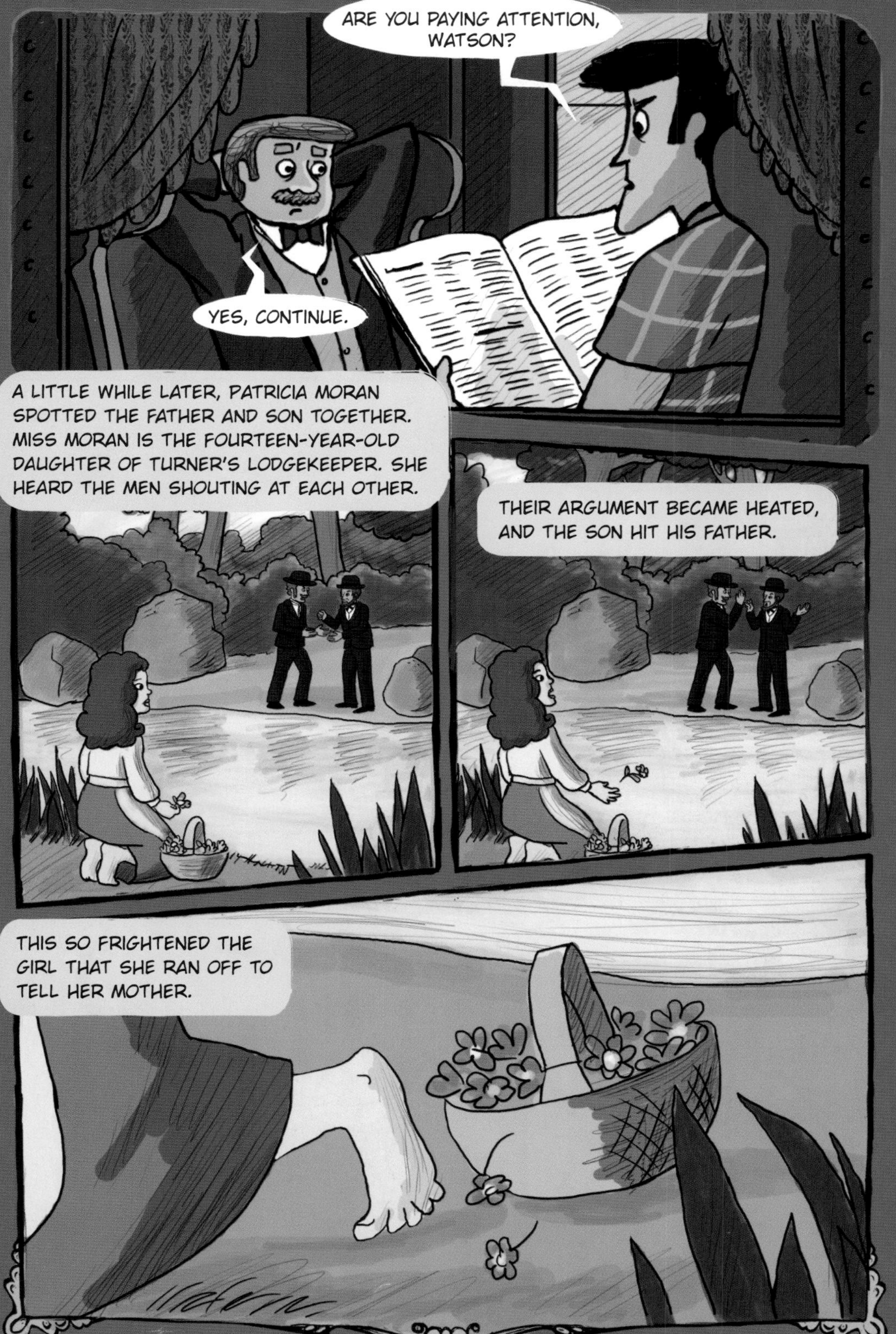
ARE YOU PAYING ATTENTION, WATSON?
YES, CONTINUE.
A LITTLE WHILE LATER, PATRICIA MORAN SPOTTED THE FATHER AND SON TOGETHER. MISS MORAN IS THE FOURTEEN-YEAR-OLD DAUGHTER OF TURNER'S LODGEKEEPER. SHE HEARD THE MEN SHOUTING AT EACH OTHER.
THEIR ARGUMENT BECAME HEATED, AND THE SON HIT HIS FATHER.
THIS SO FRIGHTENED THE GIRL THAT SHE RAN OFF TO TELL HER MOTHER.

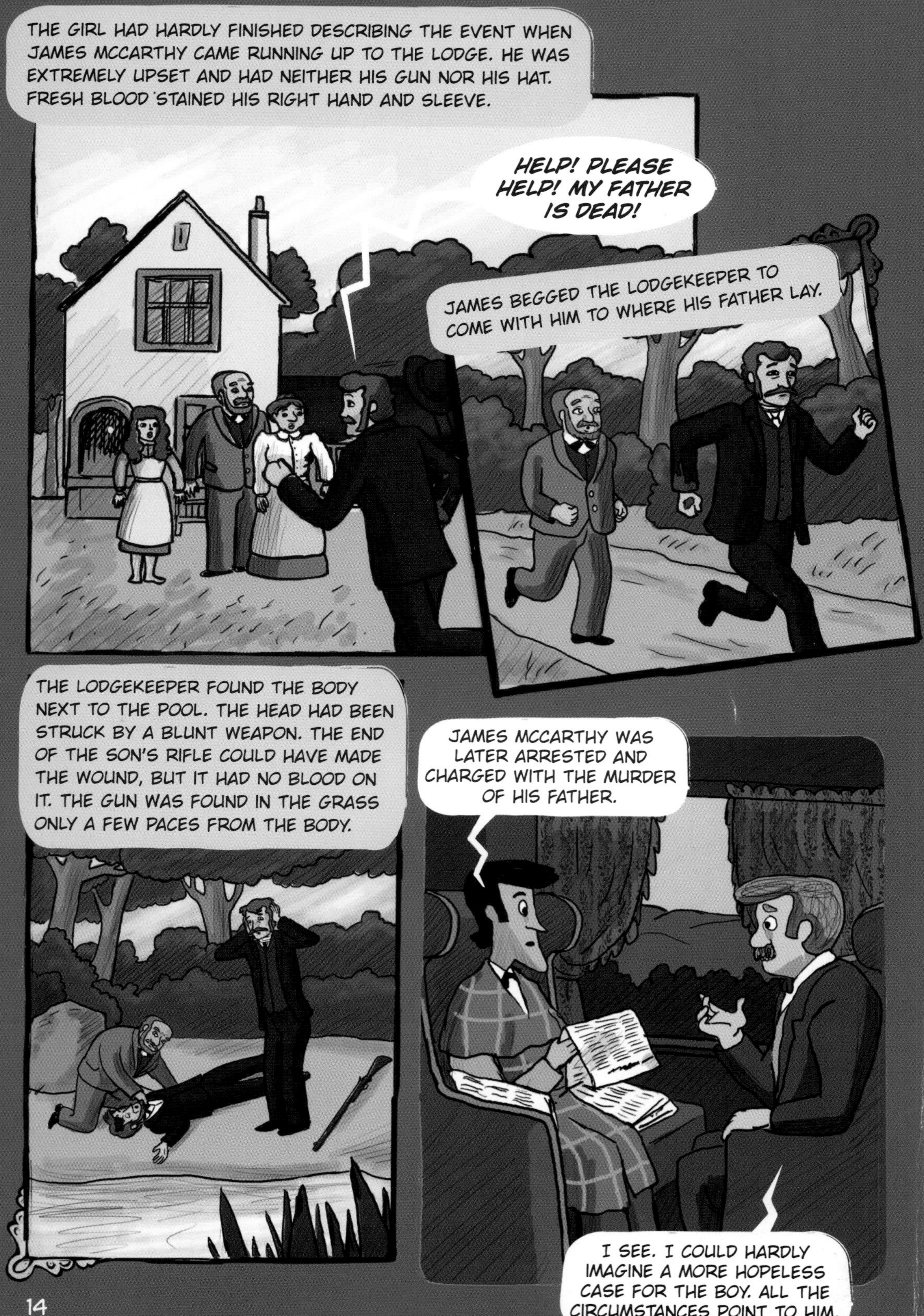
THE GIRL HAD HARDLY FINISHED DESCRIBING THE EVENT WHEN JAMES MCCARTHY CAME RUNNING UP TO THE LODGE. HE WAS EXTREMELY UPSET AND HAD NEITHER HIS GUN NOR HIS HAT. FRESH BLOOD STAINED HIS RIGHT HAND AND SLEEVE.
HELP! PLEASE HELP! MY FATHER IS DEAD!
JAMES BEGGED THE LODGEKEEPER TO COME WITH HIM TO WHERE HIS FATHER LAY.
THE LODGEKEEPER FOUND THE BODY NEXT TO THE POOL. THE HEAD HAD BEEN STRUCK BY A BLUNT WEAPON. THE END OF THE SON'S RIFLE COULD HAVE MADE THE WOUND, BUT IT HAD NO BLOOD ON IT. THE GUN WAS FOUND IN THE GRASS ONLY A FEW PACES FROM THE BODY.
JAMES MCCARTHY WAS LATER ARRESTED AND CHARGED WITH THE MURDER OF HIS FATHER.
I SEE. I COULD HARDLY IMAGINE A MORE HOPELESS CASE FOR THE BOY. ALL THE CIRCUMSTANCES POINT TO HIM.

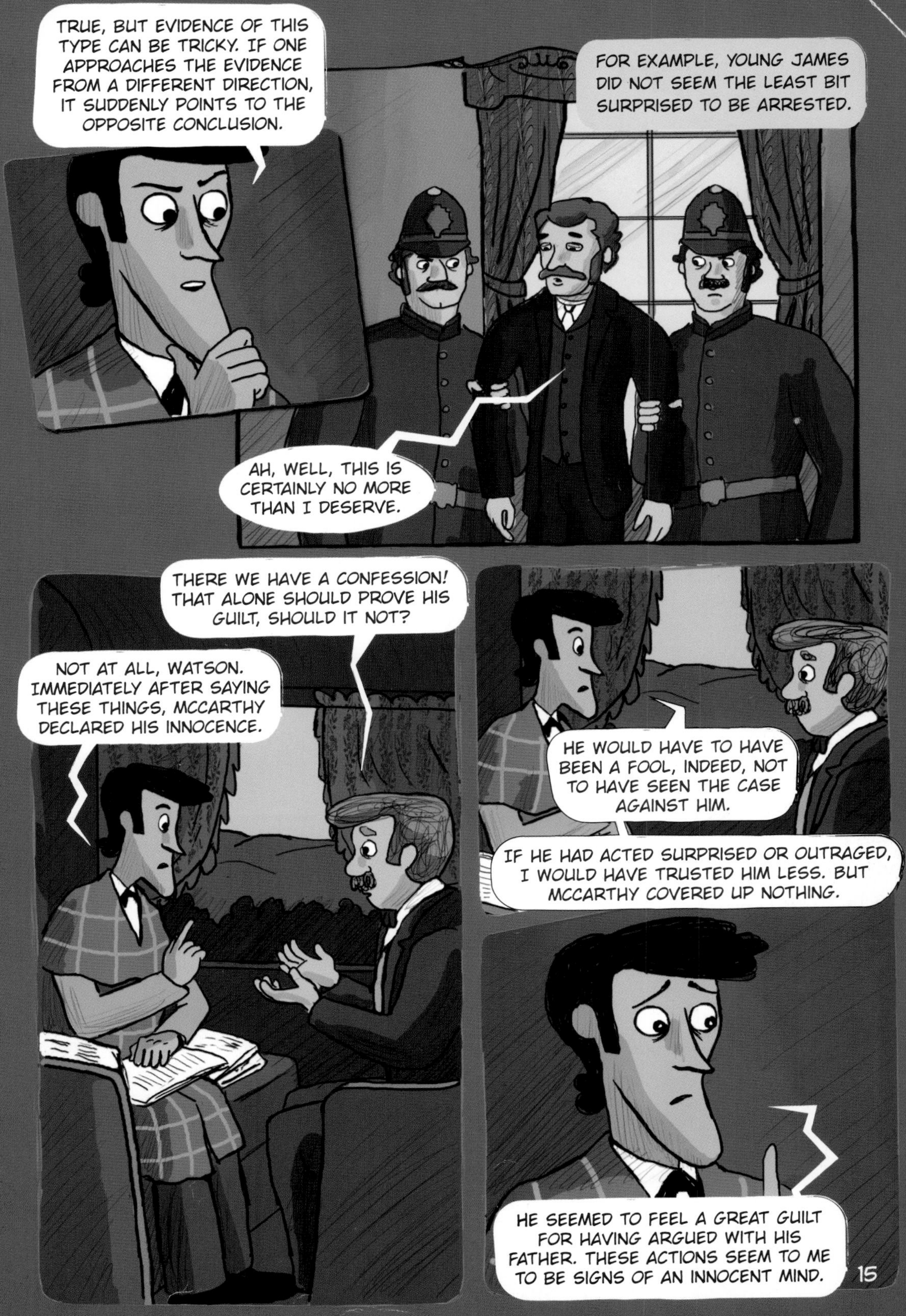
TRUE, BUT EVIDENCE OF THIS TYPE CAN BE TRICKY. IF ONE APPROACHES THE EVIDENCE FROM A DIFFERENT DIRECTION, IT SUDDENLY POINTS TO THE OPPOSITE CONCLUSION.
FOR EXAMPLE, YOUNG JAMES DID NOT SEEM THE LEAST BIT SURPRISED TO BE ARRESTED.
AH, WELL, THIS IS CERTAINLY NO MORE THAN I DESERVE.
THERE WE HAVE A CONFESSION! THAT ALONE SHOULD PROVE HIS GUILT, SHOULD IT NOT?
NOT AT ALL, WATSON. IMMEDIATELY AFTER SAYING THESE THINGS, MCCARTHY DECLARED HIS INNOCENCE.
HE WOULD HAVE TO HAVE BEEN A FOOL, INDEED, NOT TO HAVE SEEN THE CASE AGAINST HIM.
IF HE HAD ACTED SURPRISED OR OUTRAGED, I WOULD HAVE TRUSTED HIM LESS. BUT MCCARTHY COVERED UP NOTHING.
HE SEEMED TO FEEL A GREAT GUILT FOR HAVING ARGUED WITH HIS FATHER. THESE ACTIONS SEEM TO ME TO BE SIGNS OF AN INNOCENT MIND.

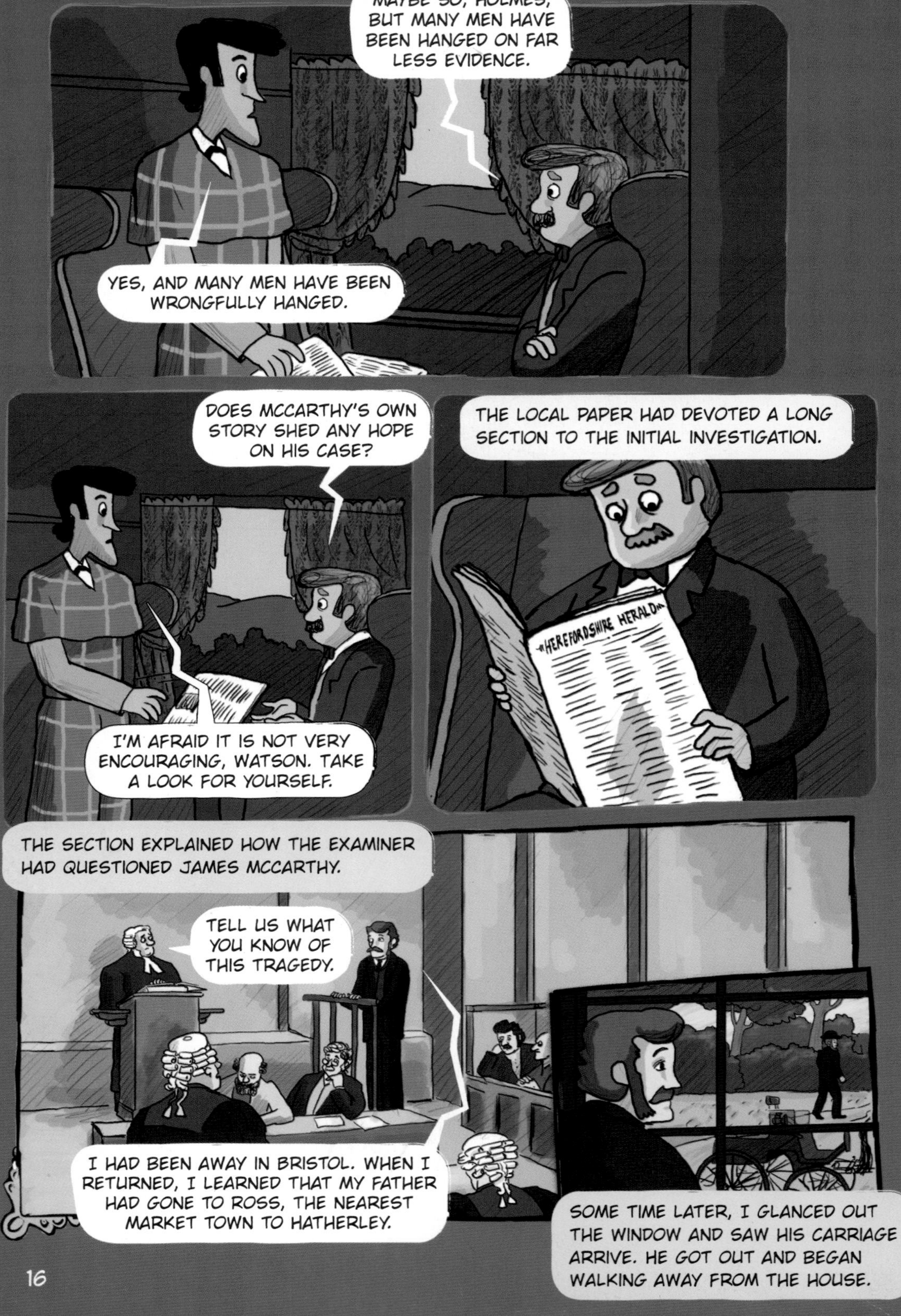
MAYBE SO, HOLMES, BUT MANY MEN HAVE BEEN HANGED ON FAR LESS EVIDENCE.
YES, AND MANY MEN HAVE BEEN WRONGFULLY HANGED.
DOES MCCARTHY'S OWN STORY SHED ANY HOPE ON HIS CASE?
I'M AFRAID IT IS NOT VERY ENCOURAGING, WATSON. TAKE A LOOK FOR YOURSELF.
THE LOCAL PAPER HAD DEVOTED A LONG SECTION TO THE INITIAL INVESTIGATION.
HEREFORDSHIRE HERALD
THE SECTION EXPLAINED HOW THE EXAMINER HAD QUESTIONED JAMES MCCARTHY.
TELL US WHAT YOU KNOW OF THIS TRAGEDY.
I HAD BEEN AWAY IN BRISTOL. WHEN I RETURNED, I LEARNED THAT MY FATHER HAD GONE TO ROSS, THE NEAREST MARKET TOWN TO HATHERLEY.
SOME TIME LATER, I GLANCED OUT THE WINDOW AND SAW HIS CARRIAGE ARRIVE. HE GOT OUT AND BEGAN WALKING AWAY FROM THE HOUSE.

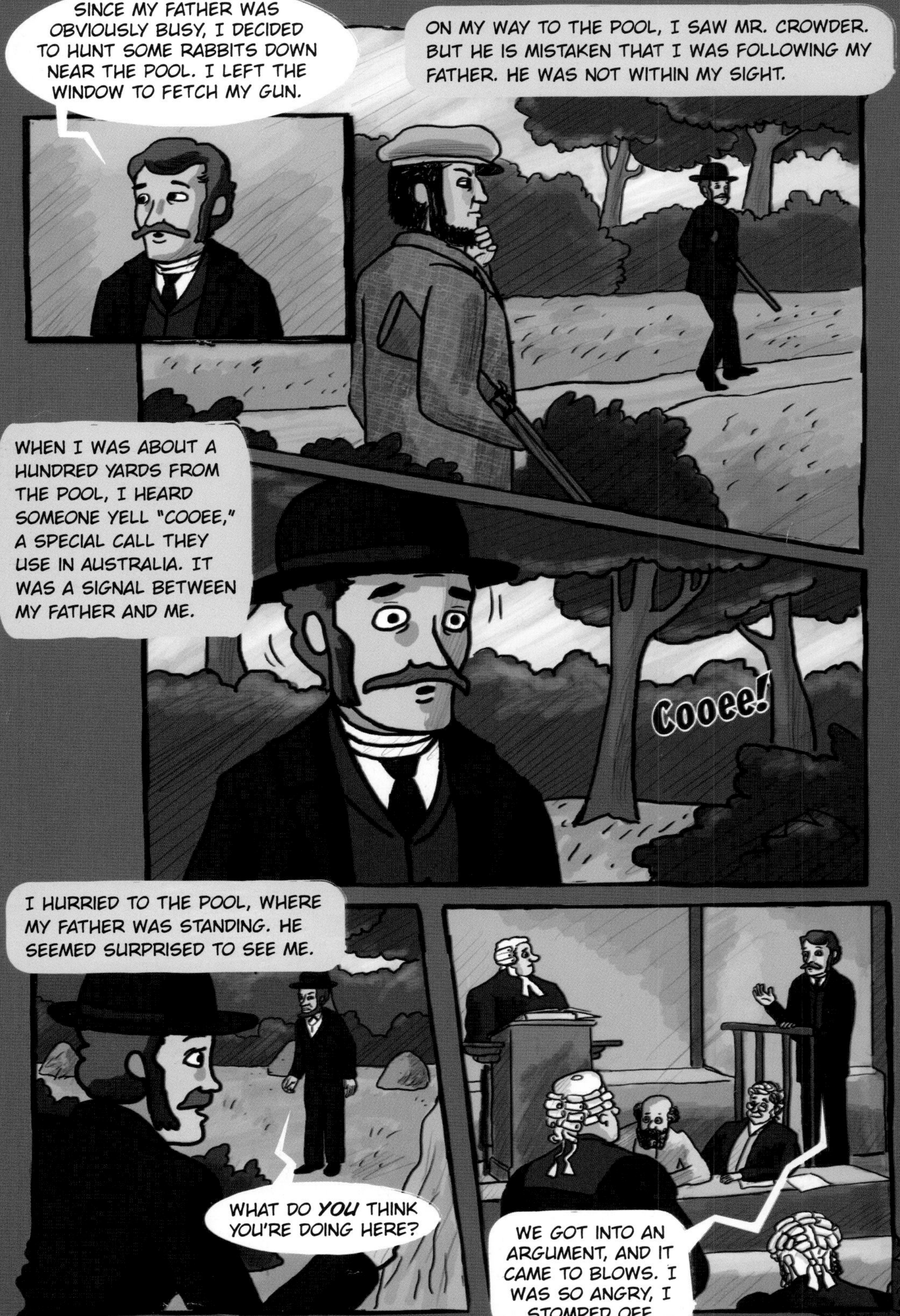
SINCE MY FATHER WAS OBVIOUSLY BUSY, I DECIDED TO HUNT SOME RABBITS DOWN NEAR THE POOL. I LEFT THE WINDOW TO FETCH MY GUN.
ON MY WAY TO THE POOL, I SAW MR. CROWDER. BUT HE IS MISTAKEN THAT I WAS FOLLOWING MY FATHER. HE WAS NOT WITHIN MY SIGHT.
WHEN I WAS ABOUT A HUNDRED YARDS FROM THE POOL, I HEARD SOMEONE YELL "COOEE," A SPECIAL CALL THEY USE IN AUSTRALIA. IT WAS A SIGNAL BETWEEN MY FATHER AND ME.
Cooee!
I HURRIED TO THE POOL, WHERE MY FATHER WAS STANDING. HE SEEMED SURPRISED TO SEE ME.
WHAT DO *YOU* THINK YOU'RE DOING HERE?
WE GOT INTO AN ARGUMENT, AND IT CAME TO BLOWS. I WAS SO ANGRY, I STOMPED OFF.

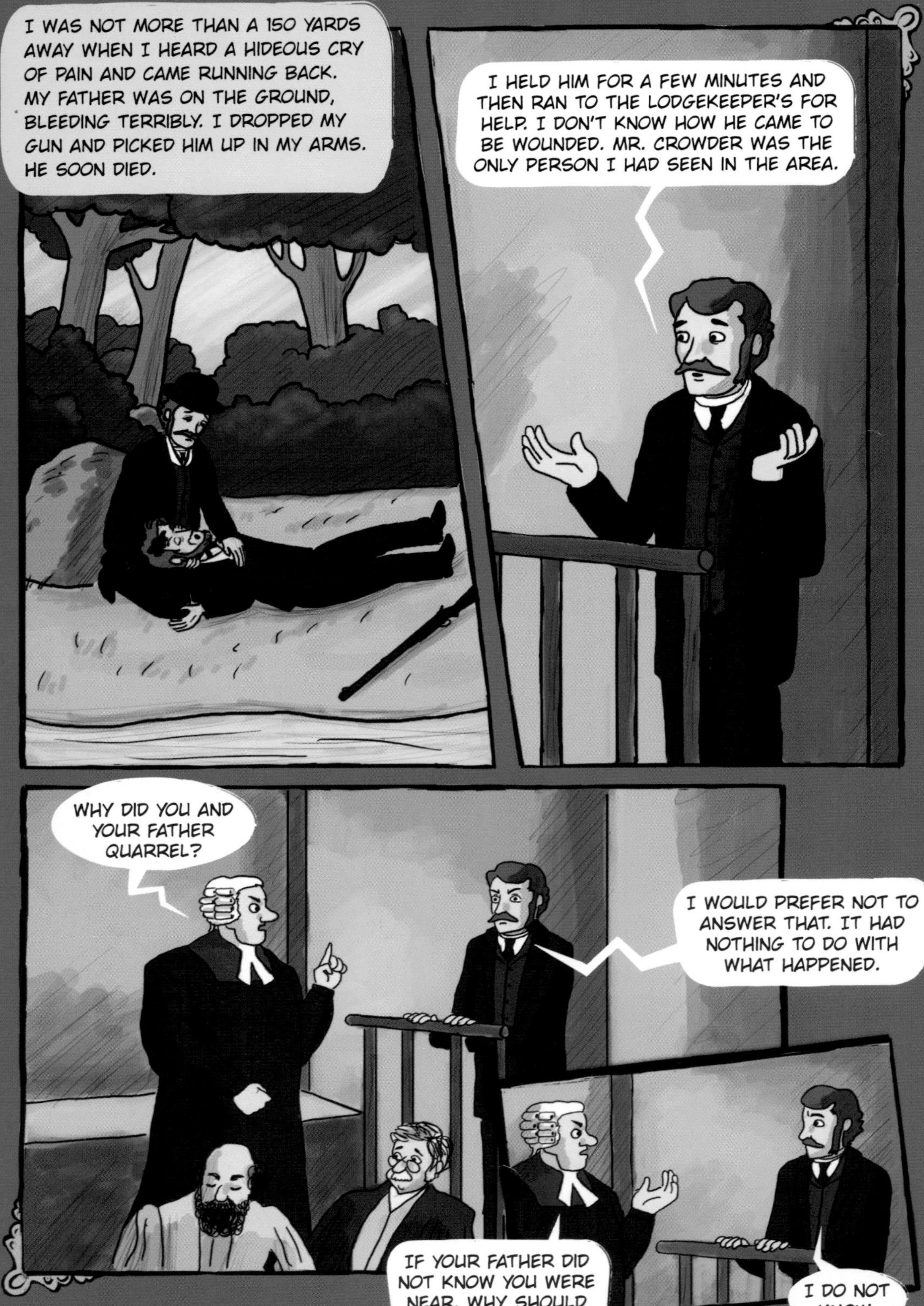
I WAS NOT MORE THAN A 150 YARDS AWAY WHEN I HEARD A HIDEOUS CRY OF PAIN AND CAME RUNNING BACK. MY FATHER WAS ON THE GROUND, BLEEDING TERRIBLY. I DROPPED MY GUN AND PICKED HIM UP IN MY ARMS. HE SOON DIED.
I HELD HIM FOR A FEW MINUTES AND THEN RAN TO THE LODGEKEEPER'S FOR HELP. I DON'T KNOW HOW HE CAME TO BE WOUNDED. MR. CROWDER WAS THE ONLY PERSON I HAD SEEN IN THE AREA.
WHY DID YOU AND YOUR FATHER QUARREL?
I WOULD PREFER NOT TO ANSWER THAT. IT HAD NOTHING TO DO WITH WHAT HAPPENED.
IF YOUR FATHER DID NOT KNOW YOU WERE NEAR, WHY SHOULD HE YELL "COOEE"?
I DO NOT KNOW.

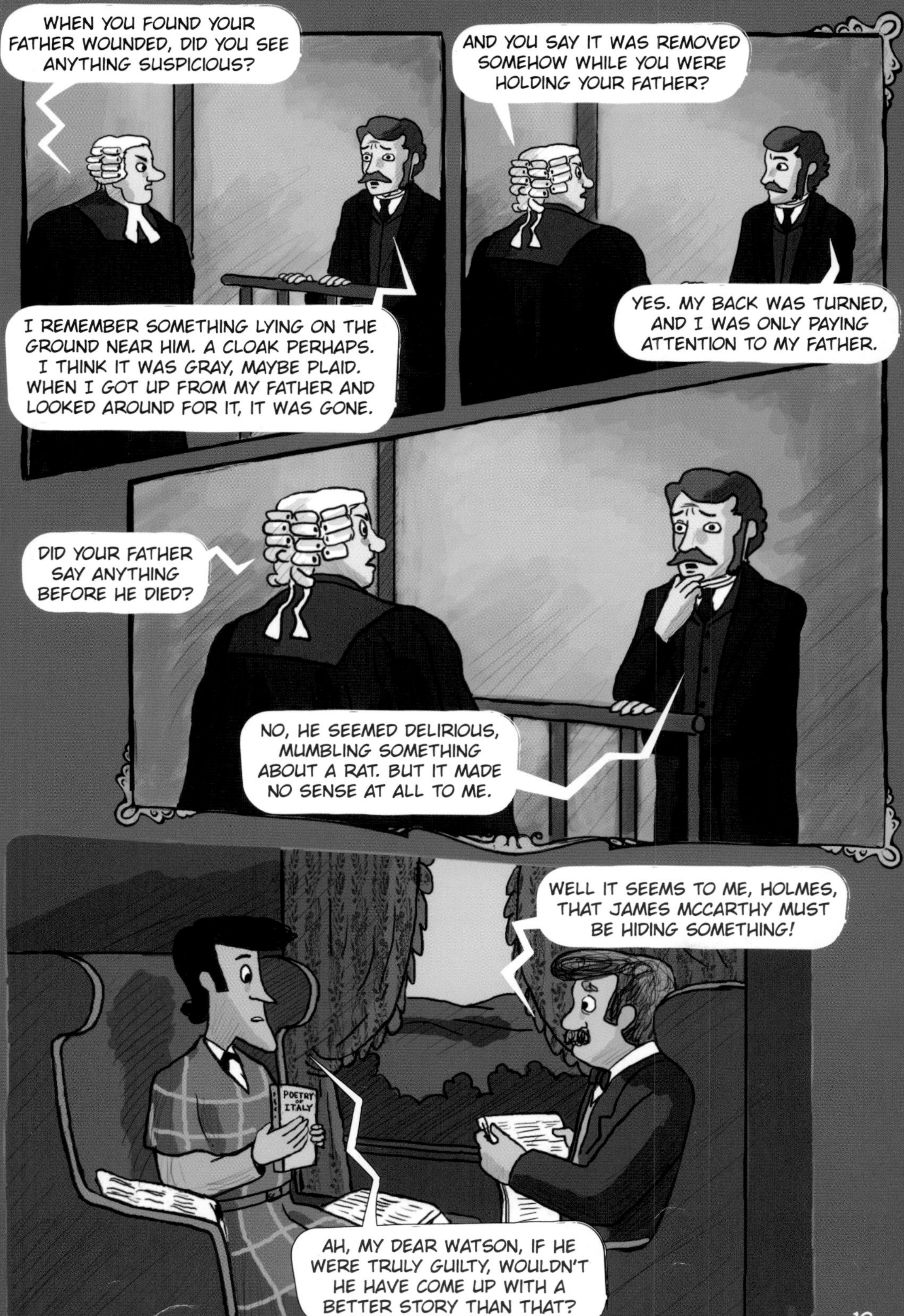
WHEN YOU FOUND YOUR FATHER WOUNDED, DID YOU SEE ANYTHING SUSPICIOUS?
I REMEMBER SOMETHING LYING ON THE GROUND NEAR HIM. A CLOAK PERHAPS. I THINK IT WAS GRAY, MAYBE PLAID. WHEN I GOT UP FROM MY FATHER AND LOOKED AROUND FOR IT, IT WAS GONE.
AND YOU SAY IT WAS REMOVED SOMEHOW WHILE YOU WERE HOLDING YOUR FATHER?
YES. MY BACK WAS TURNED, AND I WAS ONLY PAYING ATTENTION TO MY FATHER.
DID YOUR FATHER SAY ANYTHING BEFORE HE DIED?
NO, HE SEEMED DELIRIOUS, MUMBLING SOMETHING ABOUT A RAT. BUT IT MADE NO SENSE AT ALL TO ME.
WELL IT SEEMS TO ME, HOLMES, THAT JAMES MCCARTHY MUST BE HIDING SOMETHING!
POETRY OF ITALY
AH, MY DEAR WATSON, IF HE WERE TRULY GUILTY, WOULDN'T HE HAVE COME UP WITH A BETTER STORY THAN THAT?

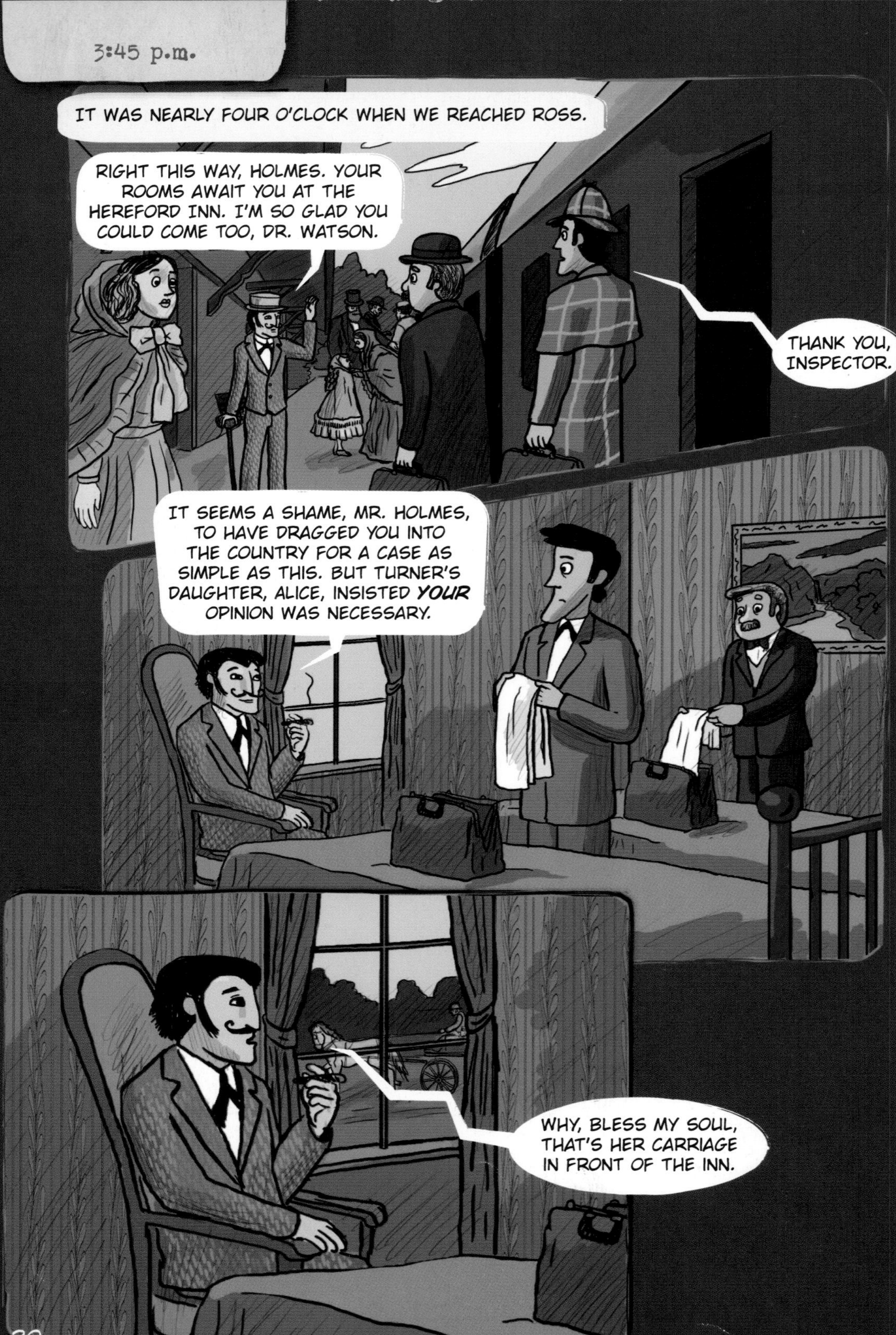
3:45 p.m.
IT WAS NEARLY FOUR O'CLOCK WHEN WE REACHED ROSS.
RIGHT THIS WAY, HOLMES. YOUR ROOMS AWAIT YOU AT THE HEREFORD INN. I'M SO GLAD YOU COULD COME TOO, DR. WATSON.
THANK YOU, INSPECTOR.
IT SEEMS A SHAME, MR. HOLMES, TO HAVE DRAGGED YOU INTO THE COUNTRY FOR A CASE AS SIMPLE AS THIS. BUT TURNER'S DAUGHTER, ALICE, INSISTED ***YOUR*** OPINION WAS NECESSARY.
WHY, BLESS MY SOUL, THAT'S HER CARRIAGE IN FRONT OF THE INN.

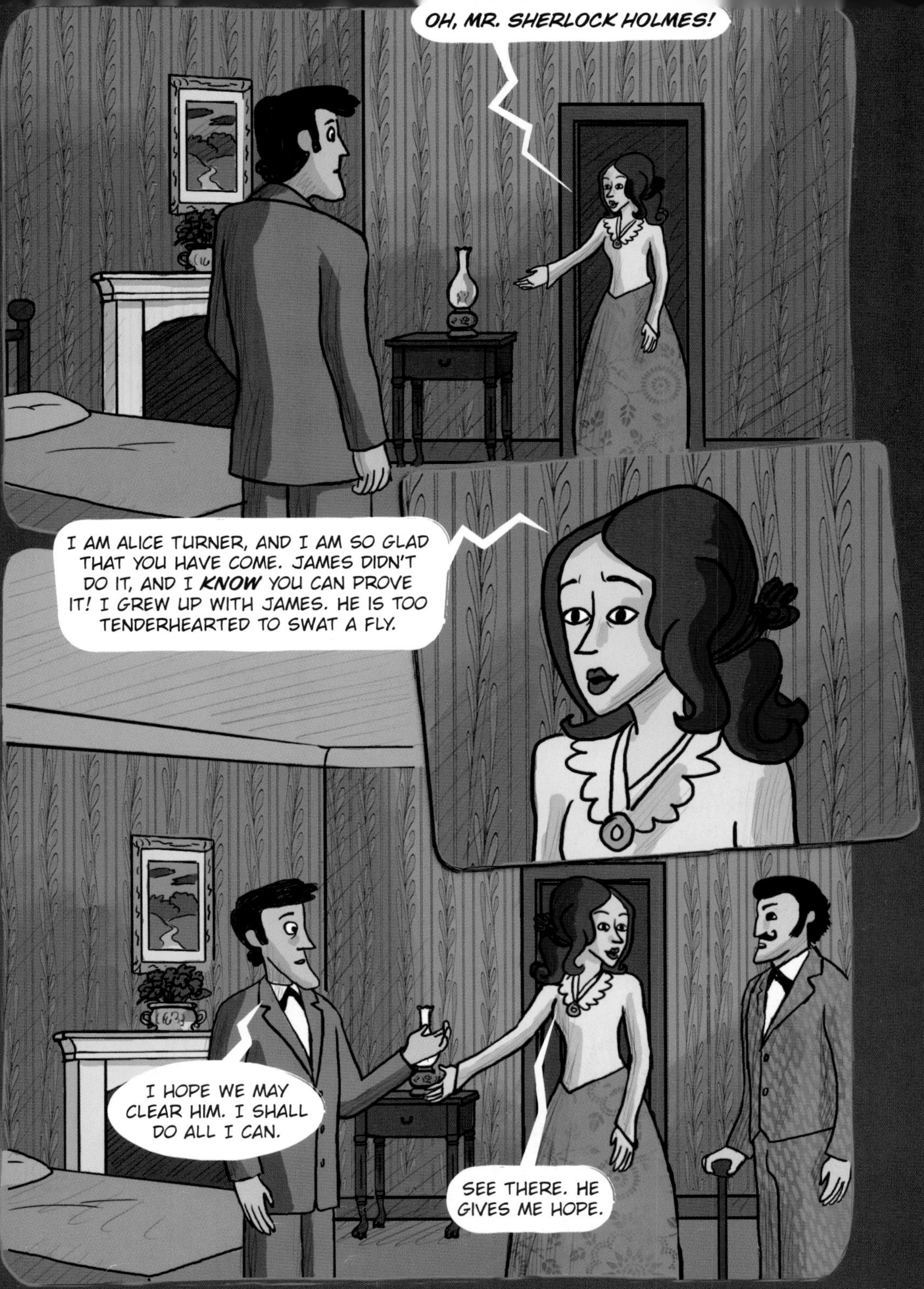
OH, MR. SHERLOCK HOLMES!
I AM ALICE TURNER, AND I AM SO GLAD THAT YOU HAVE COME. JAMES DIDN'T DO IT, AND I KNOW YOU CAN PROVE IT! I GREW UP WITH JAMES. HE IS TOO TENDERHEARTED TO SWAT A FLY.
I HOPE WE MAY CLEAR HIM. I SHALL DO ALL I CAN.
SEE THERE. HE GIVES ME HOPE.

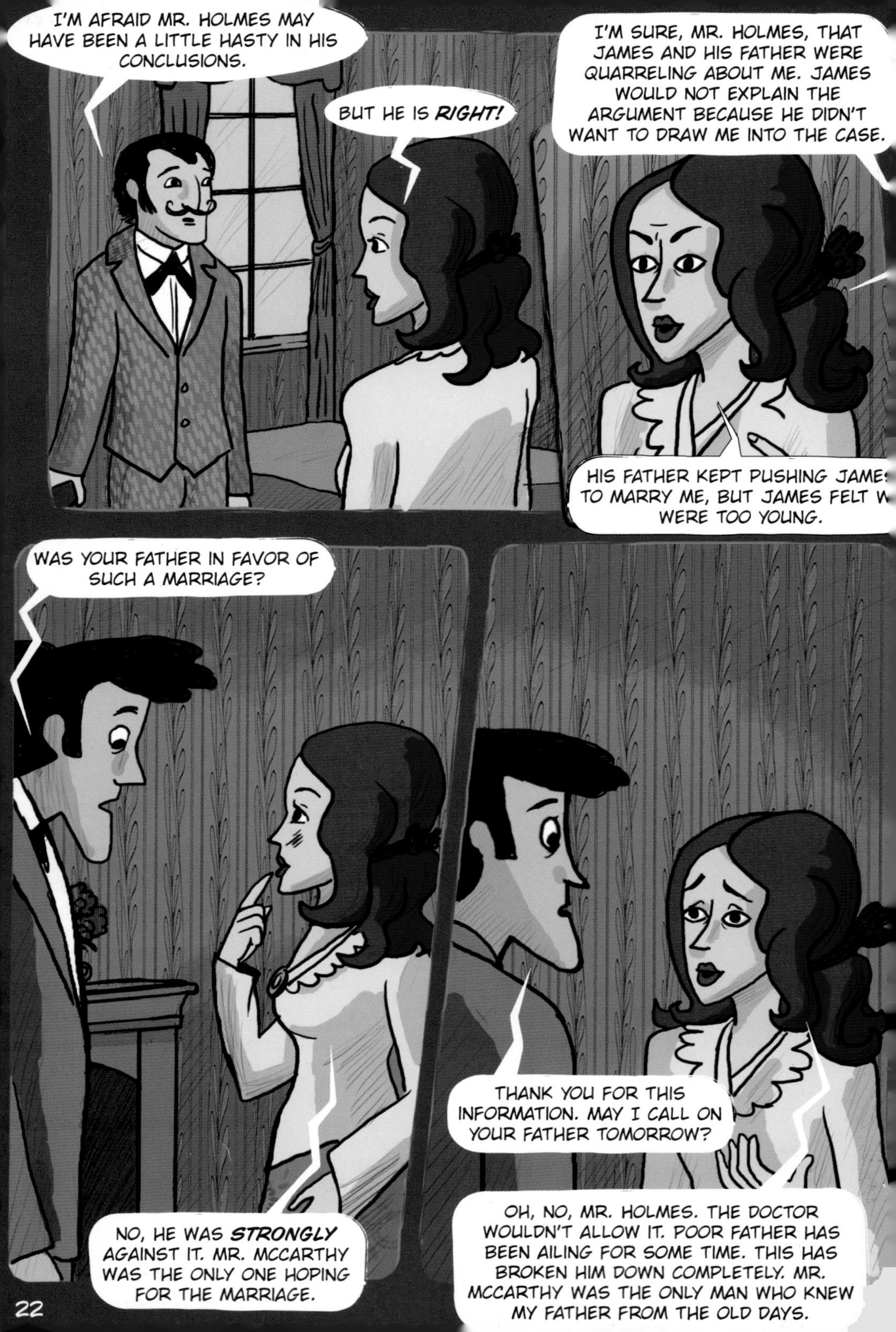
I'M AFRAID MR. HOLMES MAY HAVE BEEN A LITTLE HASTY IN HIS CONCLUSIONS.
BUT HE IS ***RIGHT!***
I'M SURE, MR. HOLMES, THAT JAMES AND HIS FATHER WERE QUARRELING ABOUT ME. JAMES WOULD NOT EXPLAIN THE ARGUMENT BECAUSE HE DIDN'T WANT TO DRAW ME INTO THE CASE.
HIS FATHER KEPT PUSHING JAMES TO MARRY ME, BUT JAMES FELT W WERE TOO YOUNG.
WAS YOUR FATHER IN FAVOR OF SUCH A MARRIAGE?
NO, HE WAS ***STRONGLY*** AGAINST IT. MR. MCCARTHY WAS THE ONLY ONE HOPING FOR THE MARRIAGE.
THANK YOU FOR THIS INFORMATION. MAY I CALL ON YOUR FATHER TOMORROW?
OH, NO, MR. HOLMES. THE DOCTOR WOULDN'T ALLOW IT. POOR FATHER HAS BEEN AILING FOR SOME TIME. THIS HAS BROKEN HIM DOWN COMPLETELY. MR. MCCARTHY WAS THE ONLY MAN WHO KNEW MY FATHER FROM THE OLD DAYS.

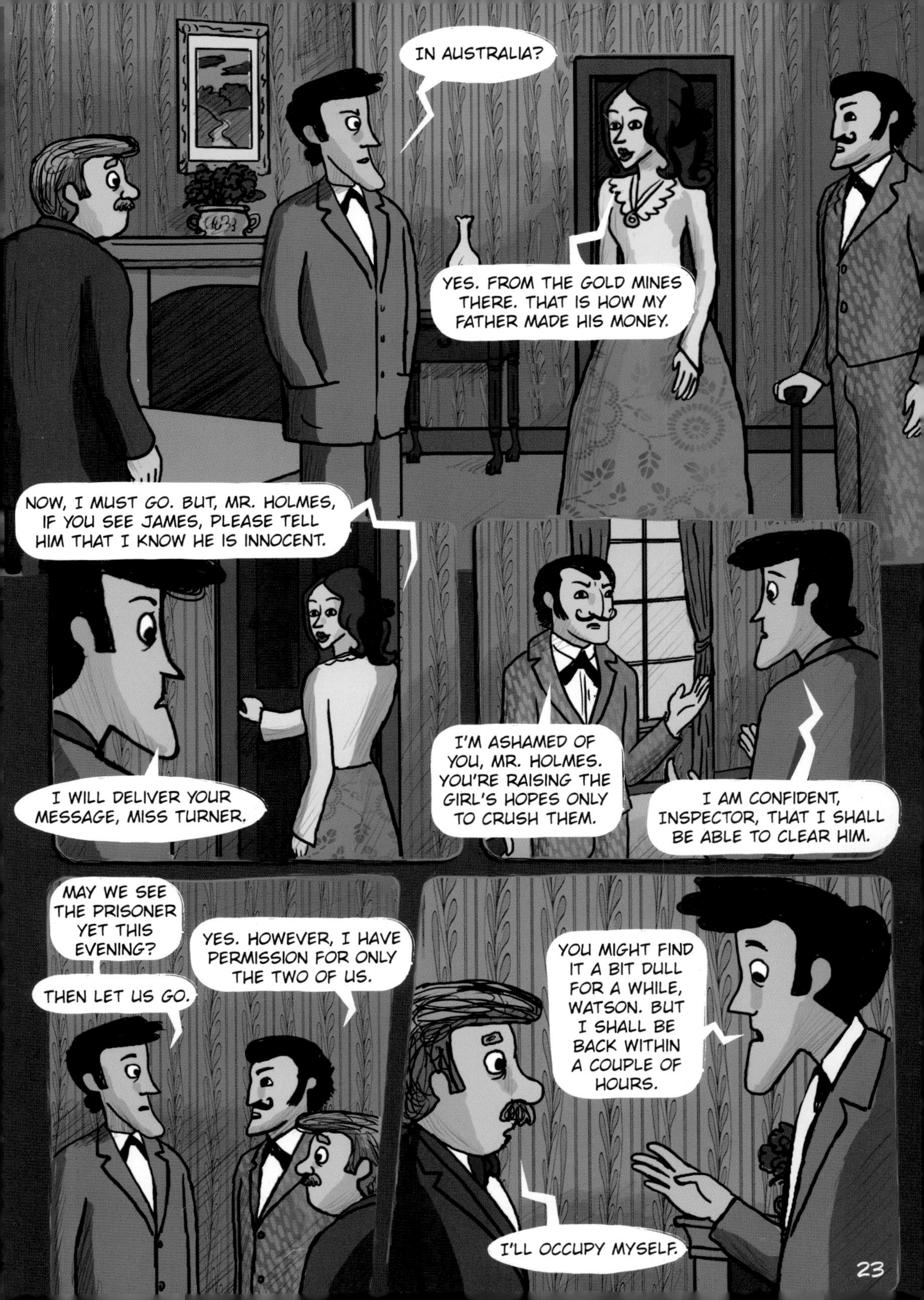
IN AUSTRALIA?
YES. FROM THE GOLD MINES THERE. THAT IS HOW MY FATHER MADE HIS MONEY.
NOW, I MUST GO. BUT, MR. HOLMES, IF YOU SEE JAMES, PLEASE TELL HIM THAT I KNOW HE IS INNOCENT.
I WILL DELIVER YOUR MESSAGE, MISS TURNER.
I'M ASHAMED OF YOU, MR. HOLMES. YOU'RE RAISING THE GIRL'S HOPES ONLY TO CRUSH THEM.
I AM CONFIDENT, INSPECTOR, THAT I SHALL BE ABLE TO CLEAR HIM.
MAY WE SEE THE PRISONER YET THIS EVENING?
YES. HOWEVER, I HAVE PERMISSION FOR ONLY THE TWO OF US.
THEN LET US GO.
YOU MIGHT FIND IT A BIT DULL FOR A WHILE, WATSON. BUT I SHALL BE BACK WITHIN A COUPLE OF HOURS.
I'LL OCCUPY MYSELF.

After they left, I tried to interest myself in a novel. But the plot seemed flat compared to the real-life story of James McCarthy. So I picked up the local paper Holmes had left. It gave a description of the injury found on McCarthy's head.

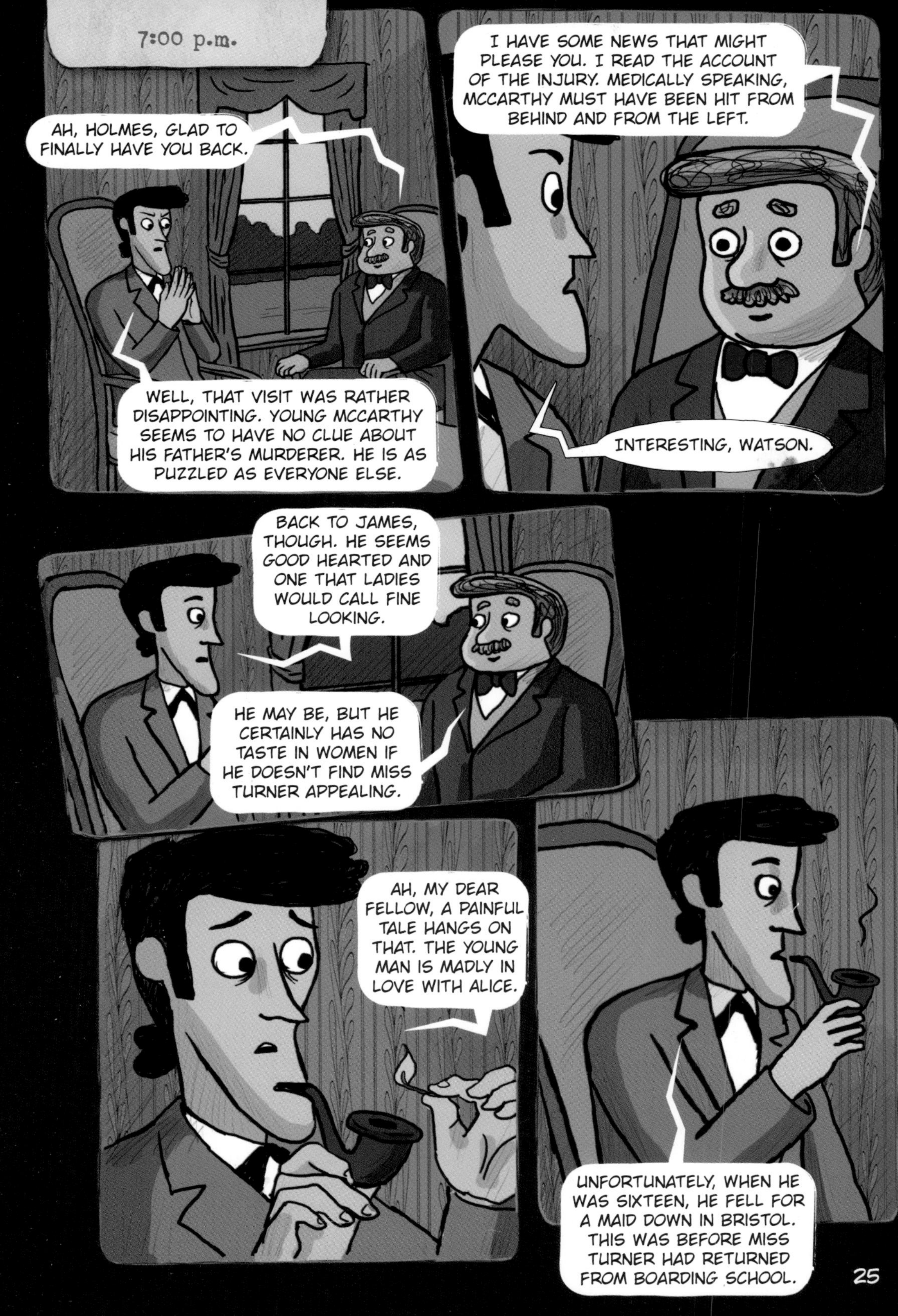
7:00 p.m.
AH, HOLMES, GLAD TO FINALLY HAVE YOU BACK.
WELL, THAT VISIT WAS RATHER DISAPPOINTING. YOUNG MCCARTHY SEEMS TO HAVE NO CLUE ABOUT HIS FATHER'S MURDERER. HE IS AS PUZZLED AS EVERYONE ELSE.
I HAVE SOME NEWS THAT MIGHT PLEASE YOU. I READ THE ACCOUNT OF THE INJURY. MEDICALLY SPEAKING, MCCARTHY MUST HAVE BEEN HIT FROM BEHIND AND FROM THE LEFT.
INTERESTING, WATSON.
BACK TO JAMES, THOUGH. HE SEEMS GOOD HEARTED AND ONE THAT LADIES WOULD CALL FINE LOOKING.
HE MAY BE, BUT HE CERTAINLY HAS NO TASTE IN WOMEN IF HE DOESN'T FIND MISS TURNER APPEALING.
AH, MY DEAR FELLOW, A PAINFUL TALE HANGS ON THAT. THE YOUNG MAN IS MADLY IN LOVE WITH ALICE.
UNFORTUNATELY, WHEN HE WAS SIXTEEN, HE FELL FOR A MAID DOWN IN BRISTOL. THIS WAS BEFORE MISS TURNER HAD RETURNED FROM BOARDING SCHOOL.

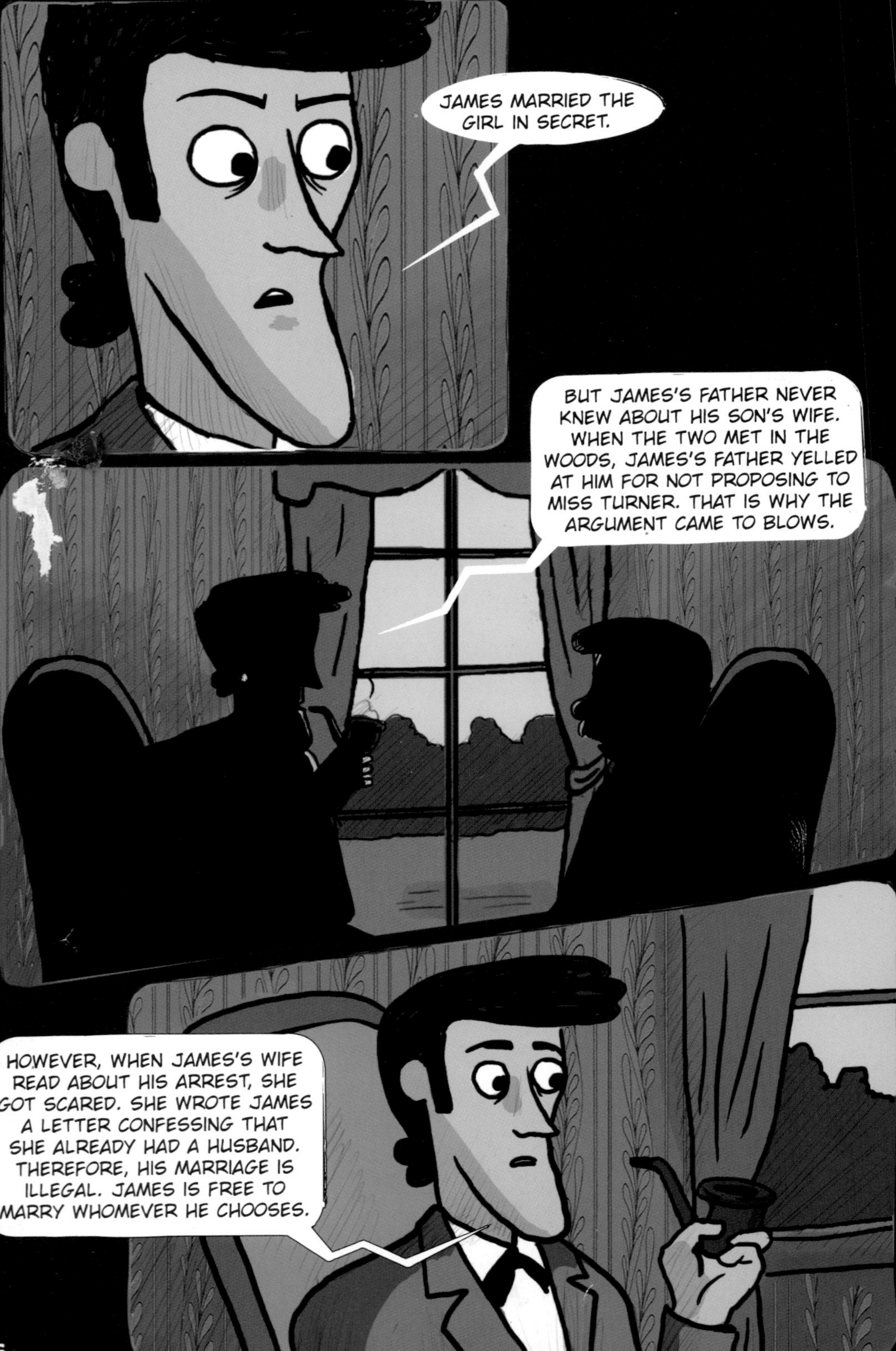
JAMES MARRIED THE GIRL IN SECRET.
BUT JAMES'S FATHER NEVER KNEW ABOUT HIS SON'S WIFE. WHEN THE TWO MET IN THE WOODS, JAMES'S FATHER YELLED AT HIM FOR NOT PROPOSING TO MISS TURNER. THAT IS WHY THE ARGUMENT CAME TO BLOWS.
HOWEVER, WHEN JAMES'S WIFE READ ABOUT HIS ARREST, SHE GOT SCARED. SHE WROTE JAMES A LETTER CONFESSING THAT SHE ALREADY HAD A HUSBAND. THEREFORE, HIS MARRIAGE IS ILLEGAL. JAMES IS FREE TO MARRY WHOMEVER HE CHOOSES.

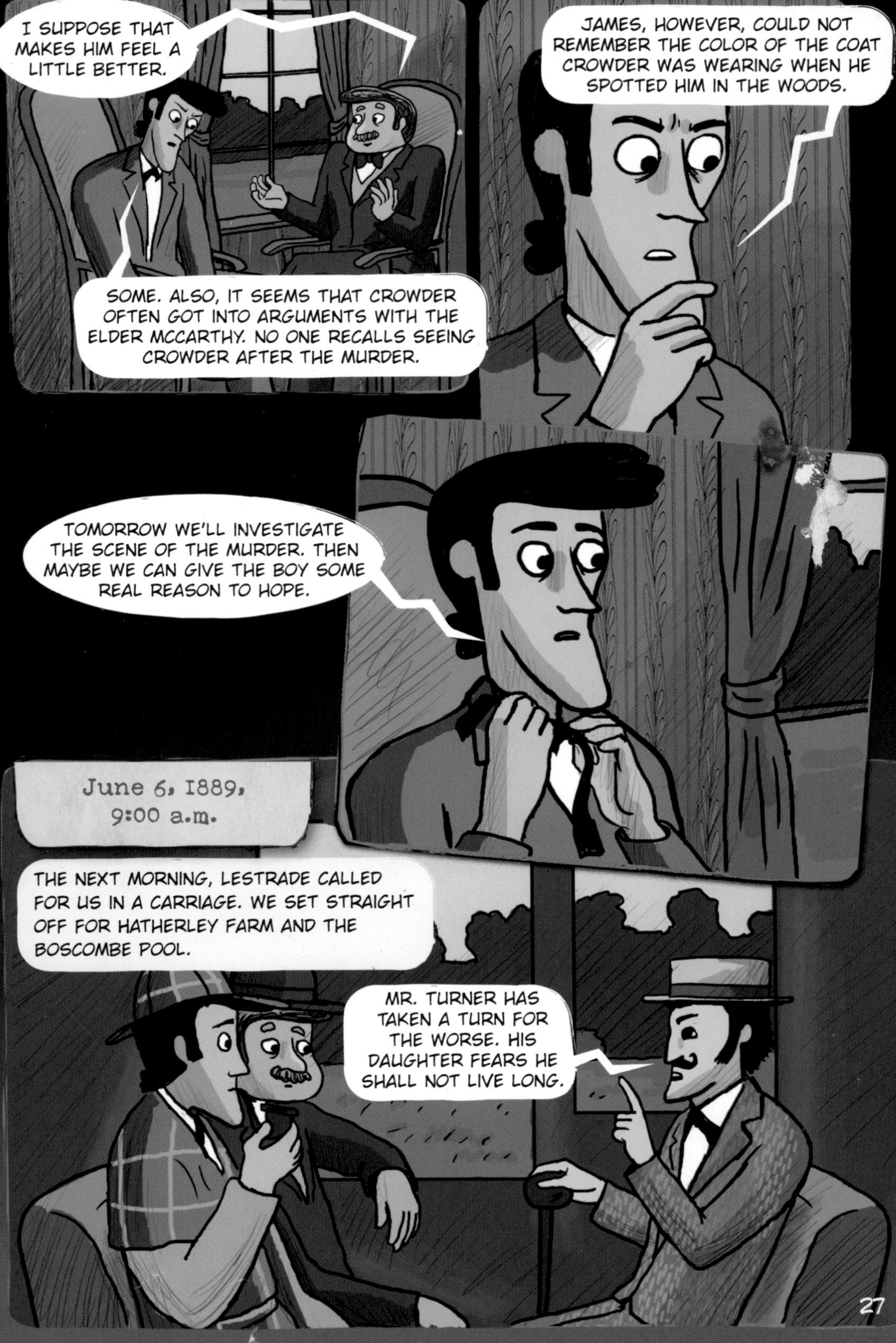
I SUPPOSE THAT MAKES HIM FEEL A LITTLE BETTER.
SOME. ALSO, IT SEEMS THAT CROWDER OFTEN GOT INTO ARGUMENTS WITH THE ELDER MCCARTHY. NO ONE RECALLS SEEING CROWDER AFTER THE MURDER.
JAMES, HOWEVER, COULD NOT REMEMBER THE COLOR OF THE COAT CROWDER WAS WEARING WHEN HE SPOTTED HIM IN THE WOODS.
TOMORROW WE'LL INVESTIGATE THE SCENE OF THE MURDER. THEN MAYBE WE CAN GIVE THE BOY SOME REAL REASON TO HOPE.
June 6, 1889, 9:00 a.m.
THE NEXT MORNING, LESTRADE CALLED FOR US IN A CARRIAGE. WE SET STRAIGHT OFF FOR HATHERLEY FARM AND THE BOSCOMBE POOL.
MR. TURNER HAS TAKEN A TURN FOR THE WORSE. HIS DAUGHTER FEARS HE SHALL NOT LIVE LONG.

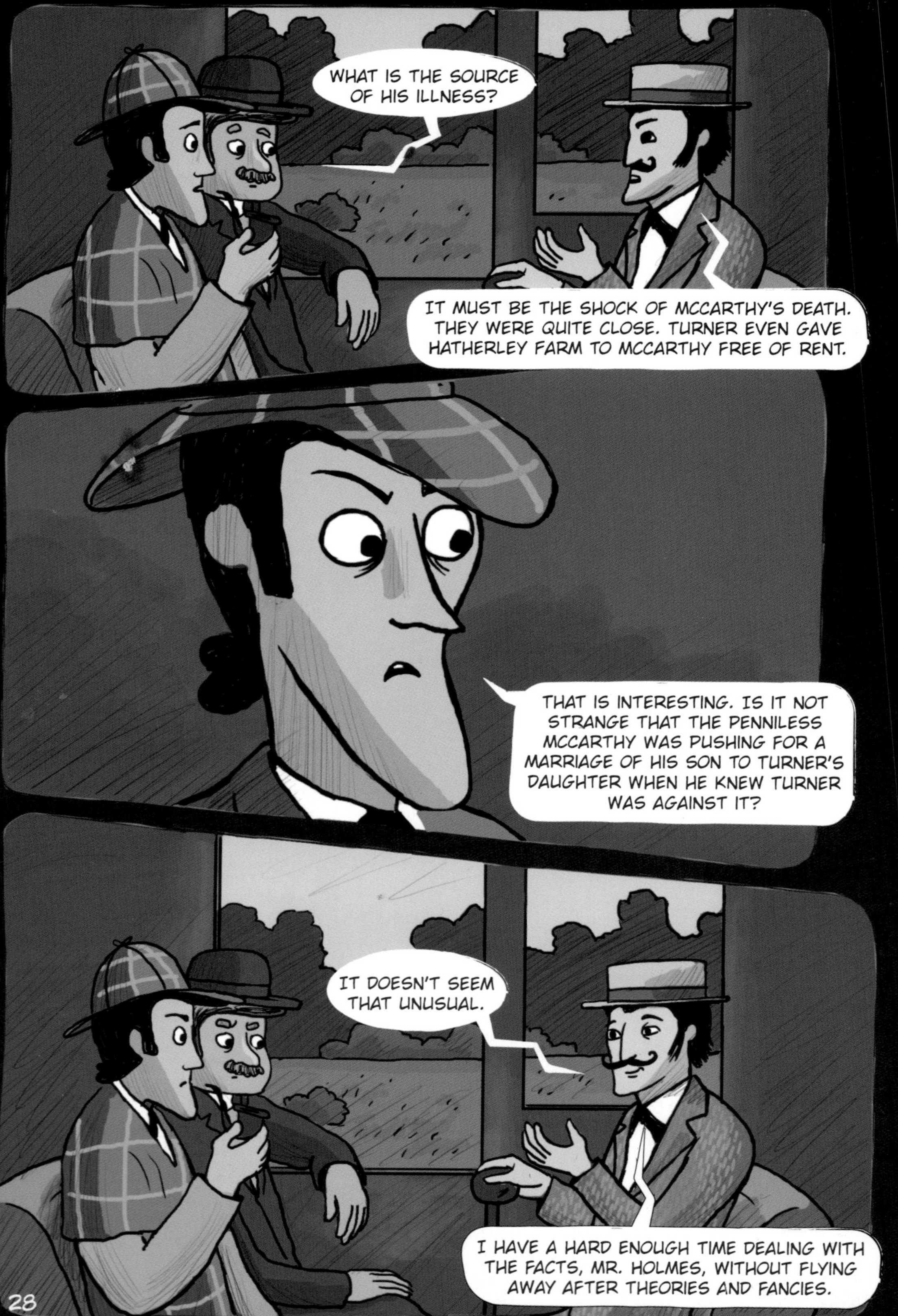
WHAT IS THE SOURCE OF HIS ILLNESS?
IT MUST BE THE SHOCK OF MCCARTHY'S DEATH. THEY WERE QUITE CLOSE. TURNER EVEN GAVE HATHERLEY FARM TO MCCARTHY FREE OF RENT.
THAT IS INTERESTING. IS IT NOT STRANGE THAT THE PENNILESS MCCARTHY WAS PUSHING FOR A MARRIAGE OF HIS SON TO TURNER'S DAUGHTER WHEN HE KNEW TURNER WAS AGAINST IT?
IT DOESN'T SEEM THAT UNUSUAL.
I HAVE A HARD ENOUGH TIME DEALING WITH THE FACTS, MR. HOLMES, WITHOUT FLYING AWAY AFTER THEORIES AND FANCIES.

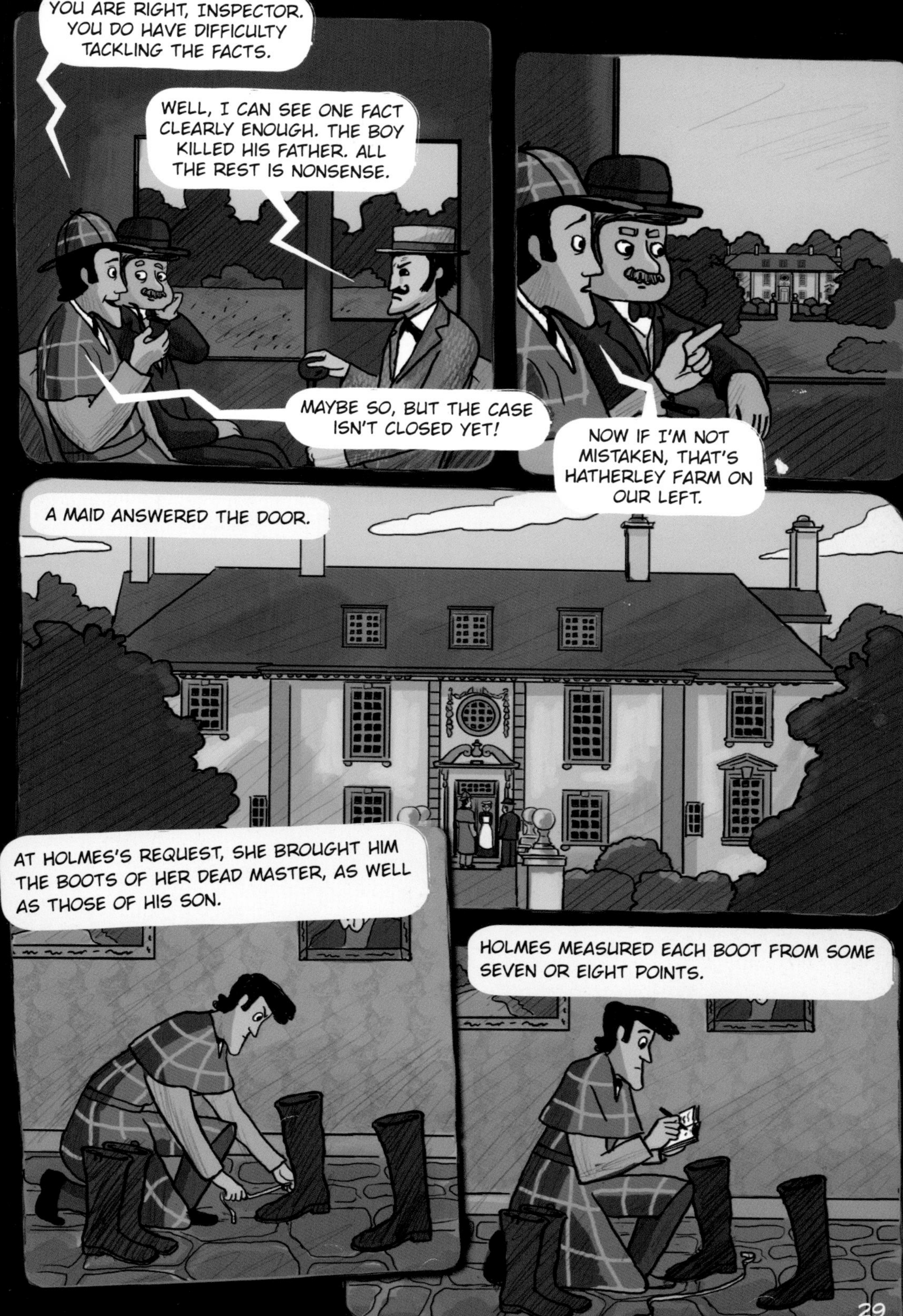

YOU ARE RIGHT, INSPECTOR. YOU DO HAVE DIFFICULTY TACKLING THE FACTS.
WELL, I CAN SEE ONE FACT CLEARLY ENOUGH. THE BOY KILLED HIS FATHER. ALL THE REST IS NONSENSE.
MAYBE SO, BUT THE CASE ISN'T CLOSED YET!
NOW IF I'M NOT MISTAKEN, THAT'S HATHERLEY FARM ON OUR LEFT.
A MAID ANSWERED THE DOOR.
AT HOLMES'S REQUEST, SHE BROUGHT HIM THE BOOTS OF HER DEAD MASTER, AS WELL AS THOSE OF HIS SON.
HOLMES MEASURED EACH BOOT FROM SOME SEVEN OR EIGHT POINTS.

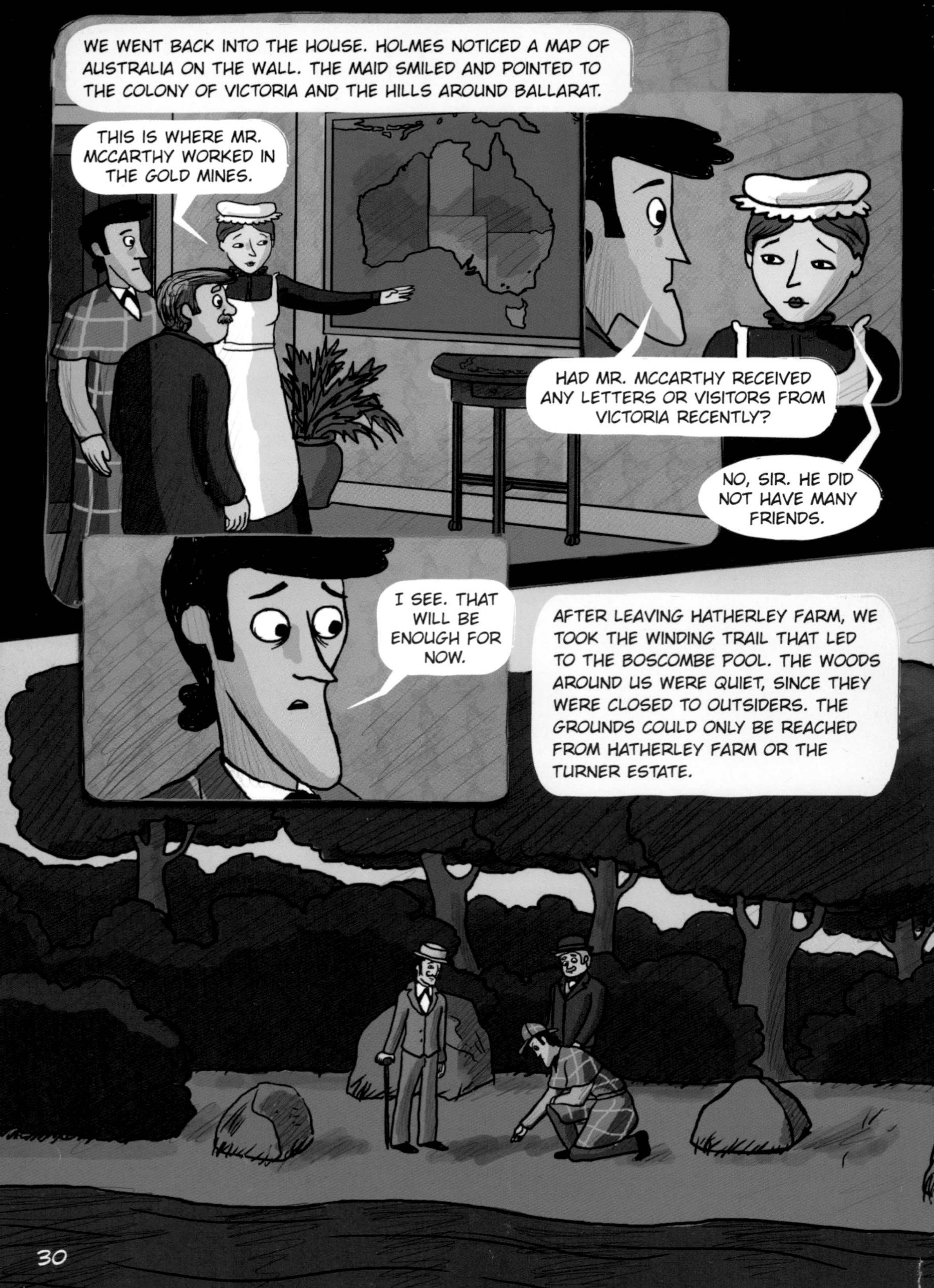
WE WENT BACK INTO THE HOUSE. HOLMES NOTICED A MAP OF AUSTRALIA ON THE WALL. THE MAID SMILED AND POINTED TO THE COLONY OF VICTORIA AND THE HILLS AROUND BALLARAT.
THIS IS WHERE MR. MCCARTHY WORKED IN THE GOLD MINES.
HAD MR. MCCARTHY RECEIVED ANY LETTERS OR VISITORS FROM VICTORIA RECENTLY?
NO, SIR. HE DID NOT HAVE MANY FRIENDS.
I SEE. THAT WILL BE ENOUGH FOR NOW.
AFTER LEAVING HATHERLEY FARM, WE TOOK THE WINDING TRAIL THAT LED TO THE BOSCOMBE POOL. THE WOODS AROUND US WERE QUIET, SINCE THEY WERE CLOSED TO OUTSIDERS. THE GROUNDS COULD ONLY BE REACHED FROM HATHERLEY FARM OR THE TURNER ESTATE.

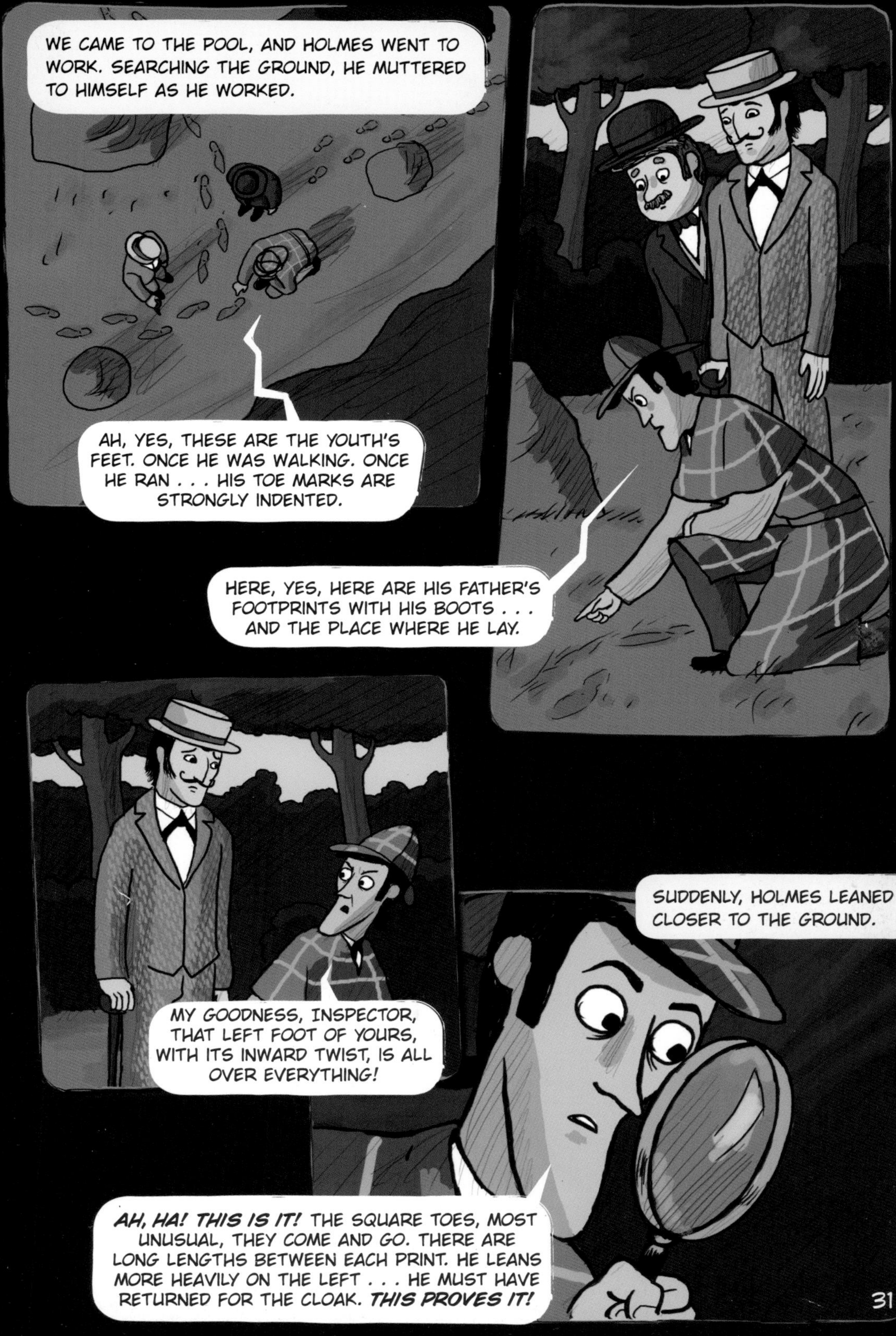
WE CAME TO THE POOL, AND HOLMES WENT TO WORK. SEARCHING THE GROUND, HE MUTTERED TO HIMSELF AS HE WORKED.
AH, YES, THESE ARE THE YOUTH'S FEET. ONCE HE WAS WALKING. ONCE HE RAN . . . HIS TOE MARKS ARE STRONGLY INDENTED.
HERE, YES, HERE ARE HIS FATHER'S FOOTPRINTS WITH HIS BOOTS . . . AND THE PLACE WHERE HE LAY.
MY GOODNESS, INSPECTOR, THAT LEFT FOOT OF YOURS, WITH ITS INWARD TWIST, IS ALL OVER EVERYTHING!
SUDDENLY, HOLMES LEANED CLOSER TO THE GROUND.
AH, HA! THIS IS IT! THE SQUARE TOES, MOST UNUSUAL, THEY COME AND GO. THERE ARE LONG LENGTHS BETWEEN EACH PRINT. HE LEANS MORE HEAVILY ON THE LEFT . . . HE MUST HAVE RETURNED FOR THE CLOAK. *THIS PROVES IT!*

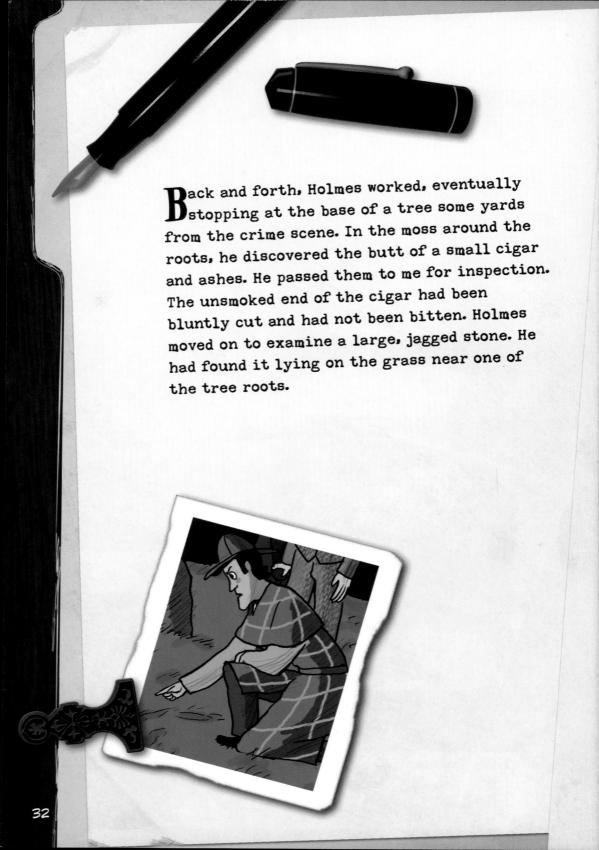

Back and forth, Holmes worked, eventually stopping at the base of a tree some yards from the crime scene. In the moss around the roots, he discovered the butt of a small cigar and ashes. He passed them to me for inspection. The unsmoked end of the cigar had been bluntly cut and had not been bitten. Holmes moved on to examine a large, jagged stone. He had found it lying on the grass near one of the tree roots.

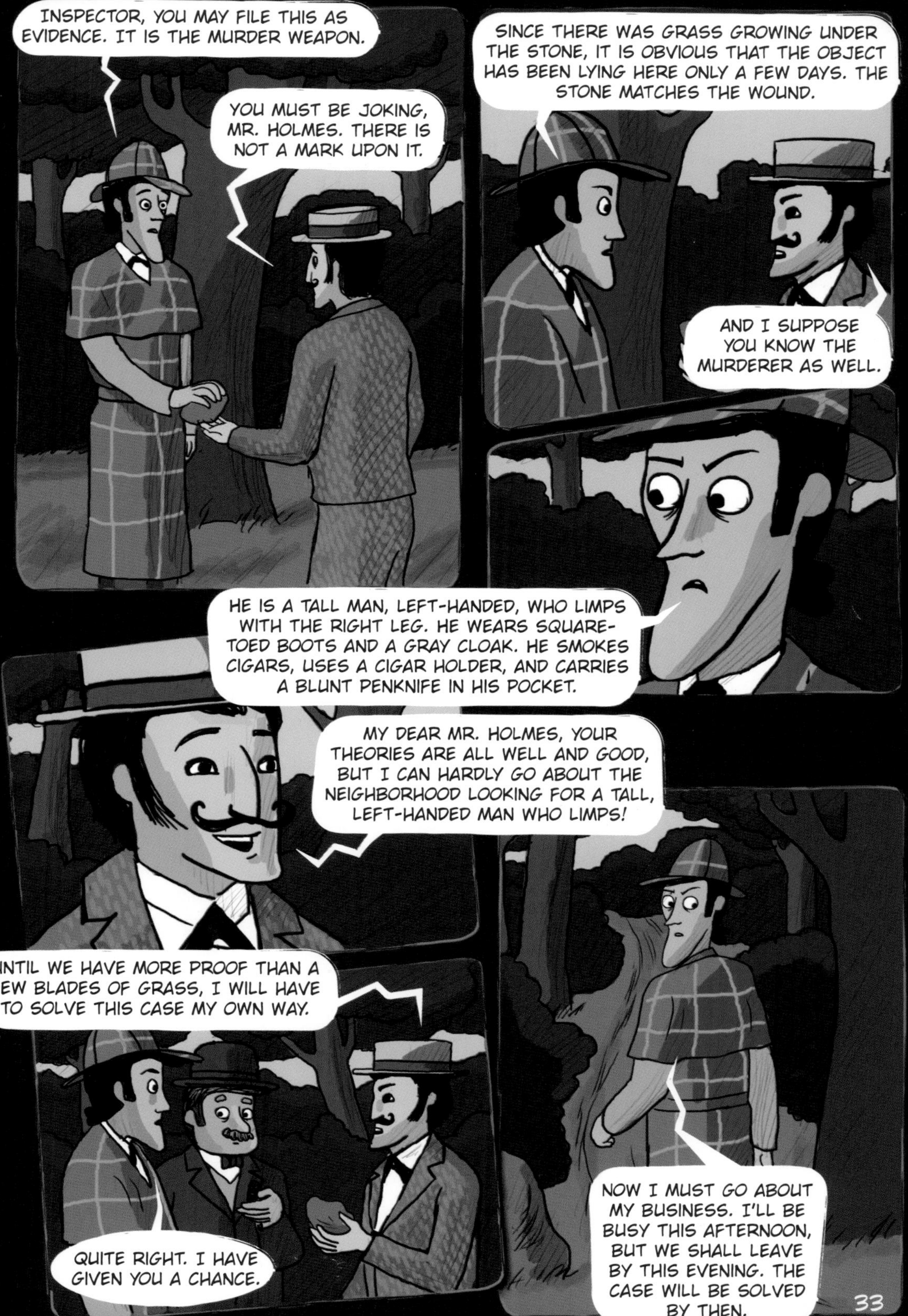
INSPECTOR, YOU MAY FILE THIS AS EVIDENCE. IT IS THE MURDER WEAPON.
YOU MUST BE JOKING, MR. HOLMES. THERE IS NOT A MARK UPON IT.
SINCE THERE WAS GRASS GROWING UNDER THE STONE, IT IS OBVIOUS THAT THE OBJECT HAS BEEN LYING HERE ONLY A FEW DAYS. THE STONE MATCHES THE WOUND.
AND I SUPPOSE YOU KNOW THE MURDERER AS WELL.
HE IS A TALL MAN, LEFT-HANDED, WHO LIMPS WITH THE RIGHT LEG. HE WEARS SQUARE-TOED BOOTS AND A GRAY CLOAK. HE SMOKES CIGARS, USES A CIGAR HOLDER, AND CARRIES A BLUNT PENKNIFE IN HIS POCKET.
MY DEAR MR. HOLMES, YOUR THEORIES ARE ALL WELL AND GOOD, BUT I CAN HARDLY GO ABOUT THE NEIGHBORHOOD LOOKING FOR A TALL, LEFT-HANDED MAN WHO LIMPS!
UNTIL WE HAVE MORE PROOF THAN A FEW BLADES OF GRASS, I WILL HAVE TO SOLVE THIS CASE MY OWN WAY.
QUITE RIGHT. I HAVE GIVEN YOU A CHANCE.
NOW I MUST GO ABOUT MY BUSINESS. I'LL BE BUSY THIS AFTERNOON, BUT WE SHALL LEAVE BY THIS EVENING. THE CASE WILL BE SOLVED BY THEN.

The inspector snickered in disbelief but said nothing more. Holmes left us in the carriage and made a quick detour on foot to the lodgekeeper's house to leave a message.

When Holmes returned, Lestrade drove us back to the inn. Holmes seemed in quite a jovial mood.

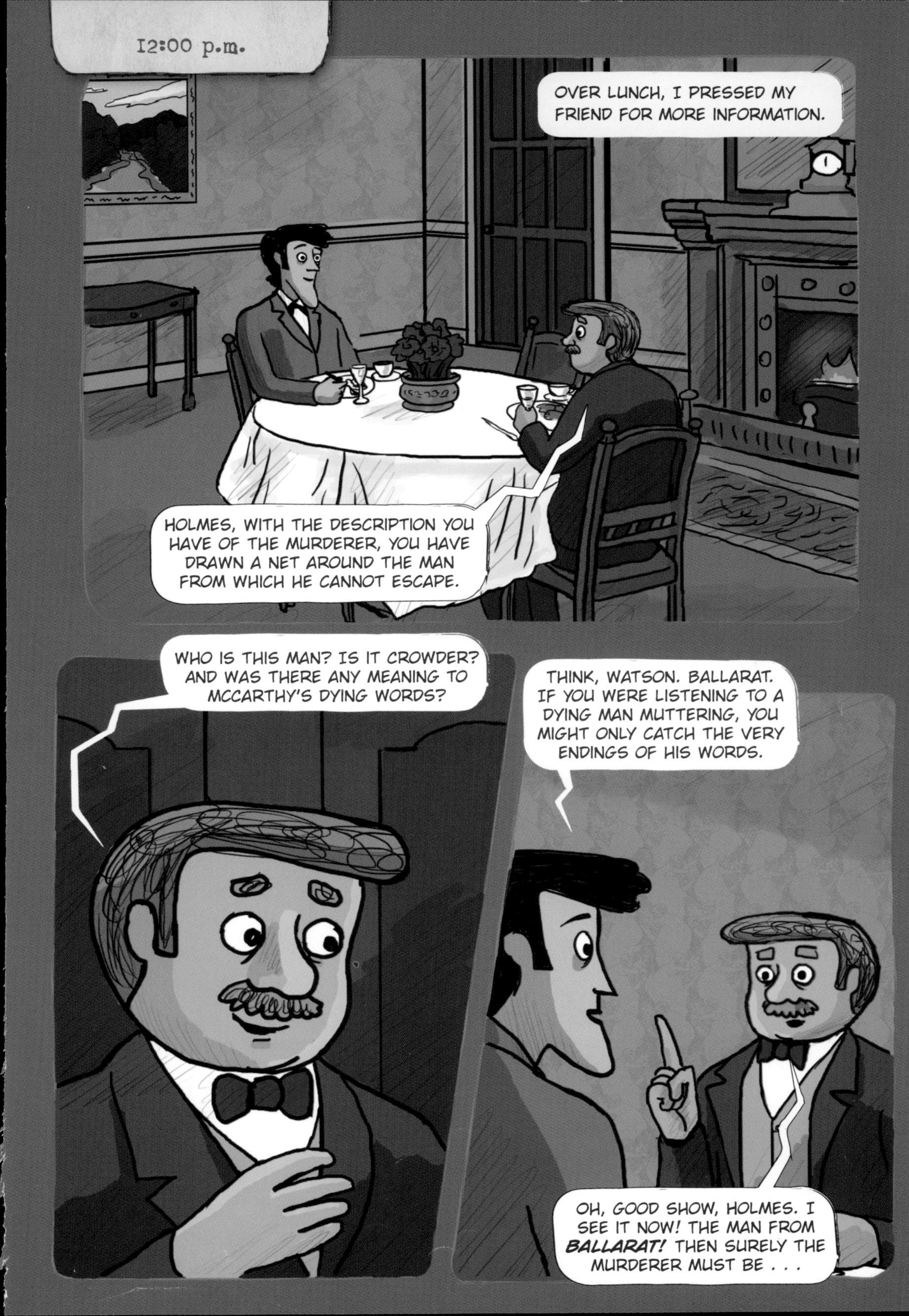
12:00 p.m.
OVER LUNCH, I PRESSED MY FRIEND FOR MORE INFORMATION.
HOLMES, WITH THE DESCRIPTION YOU HAVE OF THE MURDERER, YOU HAVE DRAWN A NET AROUND THE MAN FROM WHICH HE CANNOT ESCAPE.
WHO IS THIS MAN? IS IT CROWDER? AND WAS THERE ANY MEANING TO MCCARTHY'S DYING WORDS?
THINK, WATSON. BALLARAT. IF YOU WERE LISTENING TO A DYING MAN MUTTERING, YOU MIGHT ONLY CATCH THE VERY ENDINGS OF HIS WORDS.
OH, GOOD SHOW, HOLMES. I SEE IT NOW! THE MAN FROM ***BALLARAT!*** THEN SURELY THE MURDERER MUST BE . . .

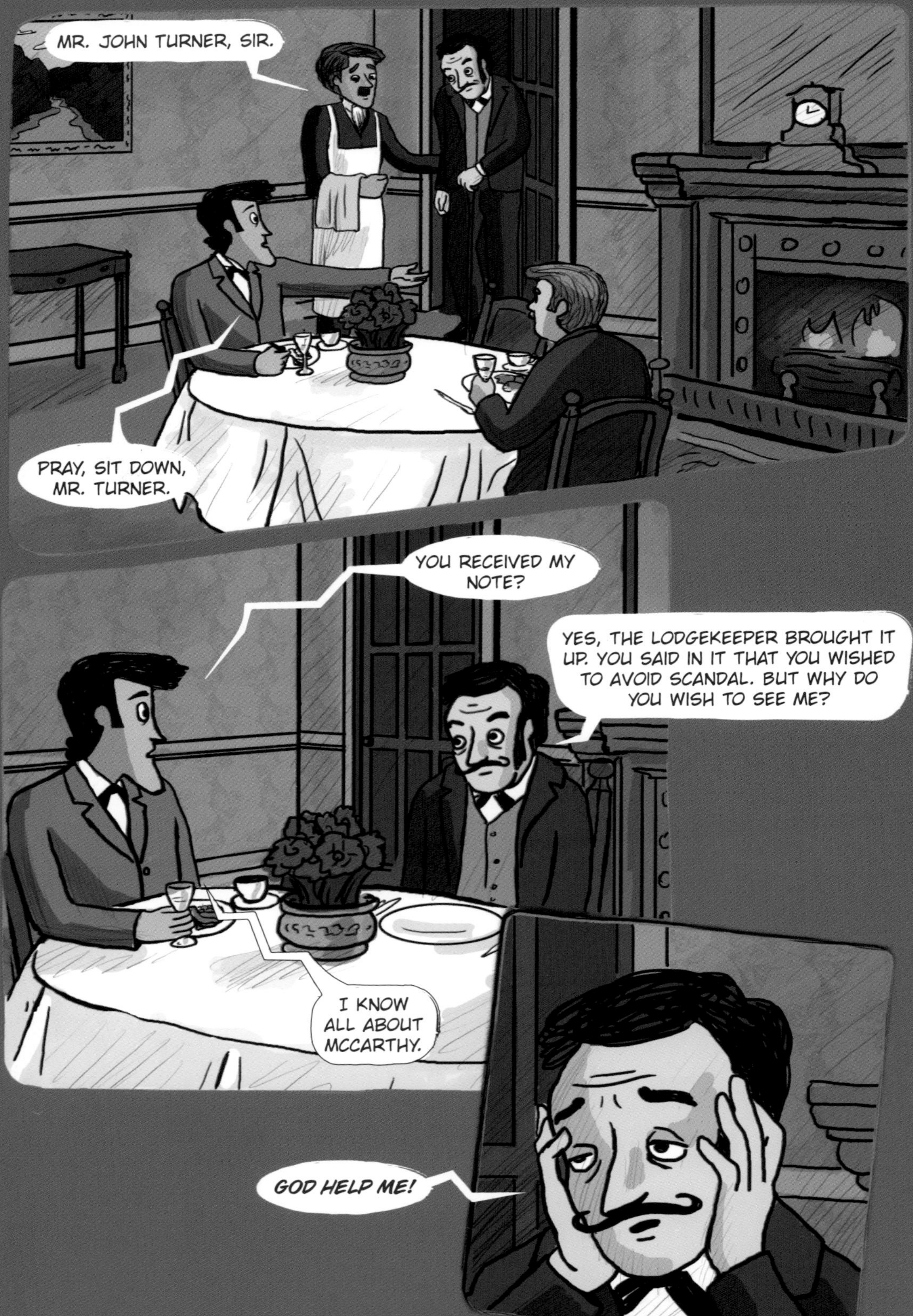
MR. JOHN TURNER, SIR.
PRAY, SIT DOWN, MR. TURNER.
YOU RECEIVED MY NOTE?
YES, THE LODGEKEEPER BROUGHT IT UP. YOU SAID IN IT THAT YOU WISHED TO AVOID SCANDAL. BUT WHY DO YOU WISH TO SEE ME?
I KNOW ALL ABOUT MCCARTHY.
GOD HELP ME!

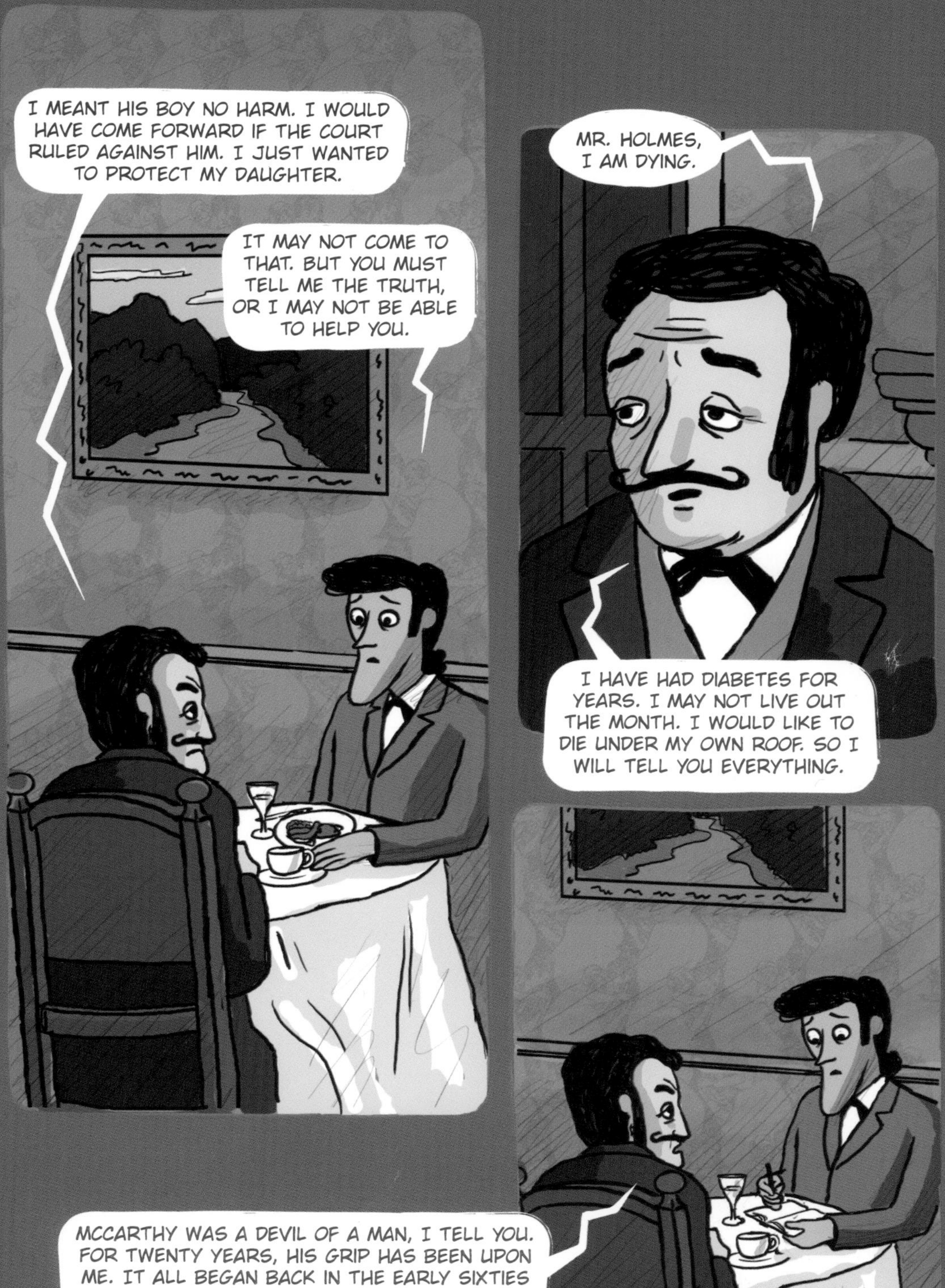

I MEANT HIS BOY NO HARM. I WOULD HAVE COME FORWARD IF THE COURT RULED AGAINST HIM. I JUST WANTED TO PROTECT MY DAUGHTER.
IT MAY NOT COME TO THAT. BUT YOU MUST TELL ME THE TRUTH, OR I MAY NOT BE ABLE TO HELP YOU.
MR. HOLMES, I AM DYING.
I HAVE HAD DIABETES FOR YEARS. I MAY NOT LIVE OUT THE MONTH. I WOULD LIKE TO DIE UNDER MY OWN ROOF. SO I WILL TELL YOU EVERYTHING.
MCCARTHY WAS A DEVIL OF A MAN, I TELL YOU. FOR TWENTY YEARS, HIS GRIP HAS BEEN UPON ME. IT ALL BEGAN BACK IN THE EARLY SIXTIES AT THE DIGGINGS IN AUSTRALIA.

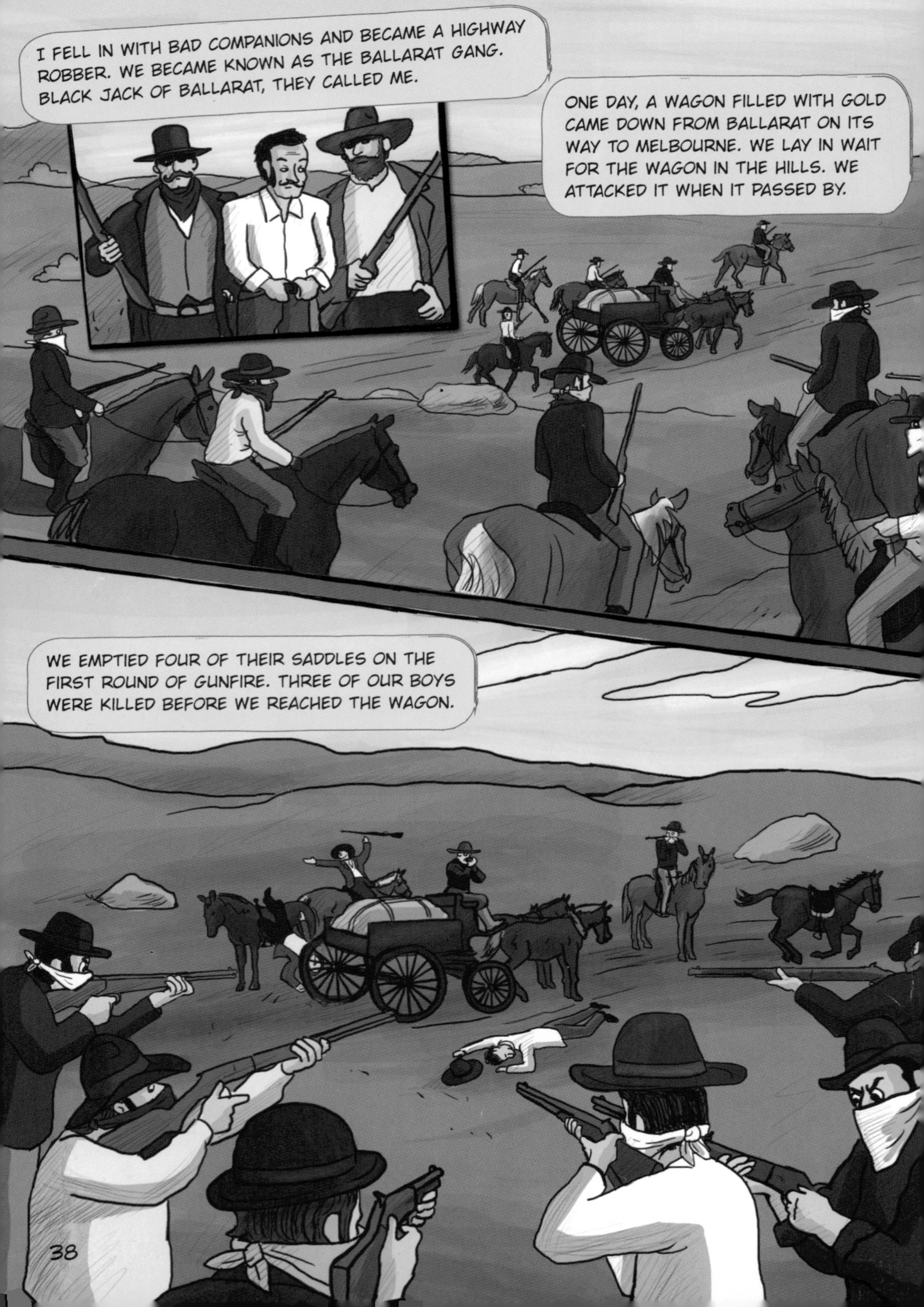
I FELL IN WITH BAD COMPANIONS AND BECAME A HIGHWAY ROBBER. WE BECAME KNOWN AS THE BALLARAT GANG. BLACK JACK OF BALLARAT, THEY CALLED ME.
ONE DAY, A WAGON FILLED WITH GOLD CAME DOWN FROM BALLARAT ON ITS WAY TO MELBOURNE. WE LAY IN WAIT FOR THE WAGON IN THE HILLS. WE ATTACKED IT WHEN IT PASSED BY.
WE EMPTIED FOUR OF THEIR SADDLES ON THE FIRST ROUND OF GUNFIRE. THREE OF OUR BOYS WERE KILLED BEFORE WE REACHED THE WAGON.

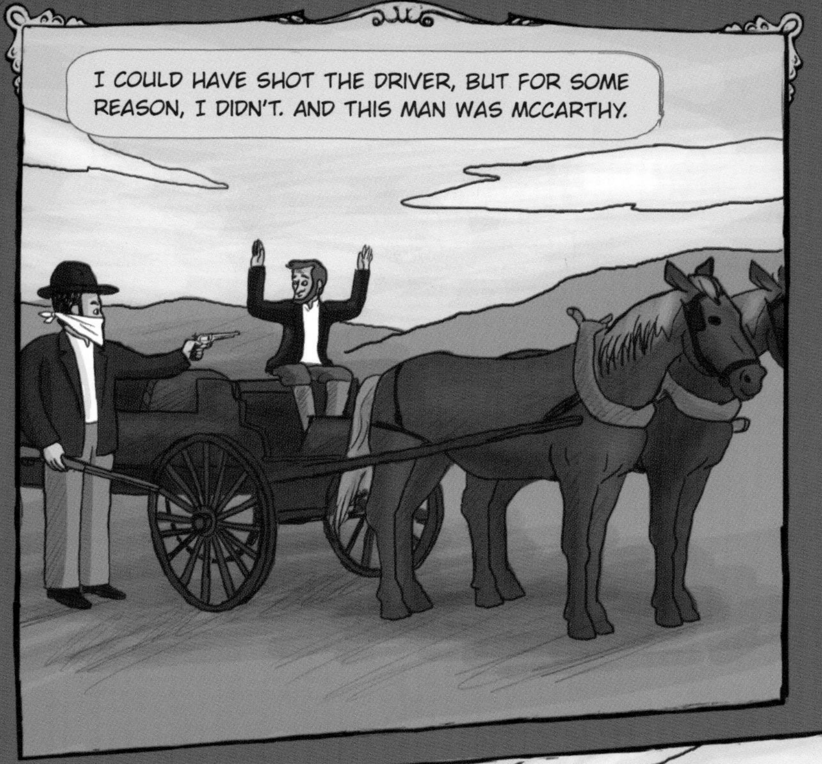
I COULD HAVE SHOT THE DRIVER, BUT FOR SOME REASON, I DIDN'T. AND THIS MAN WAS MCCARTHY.

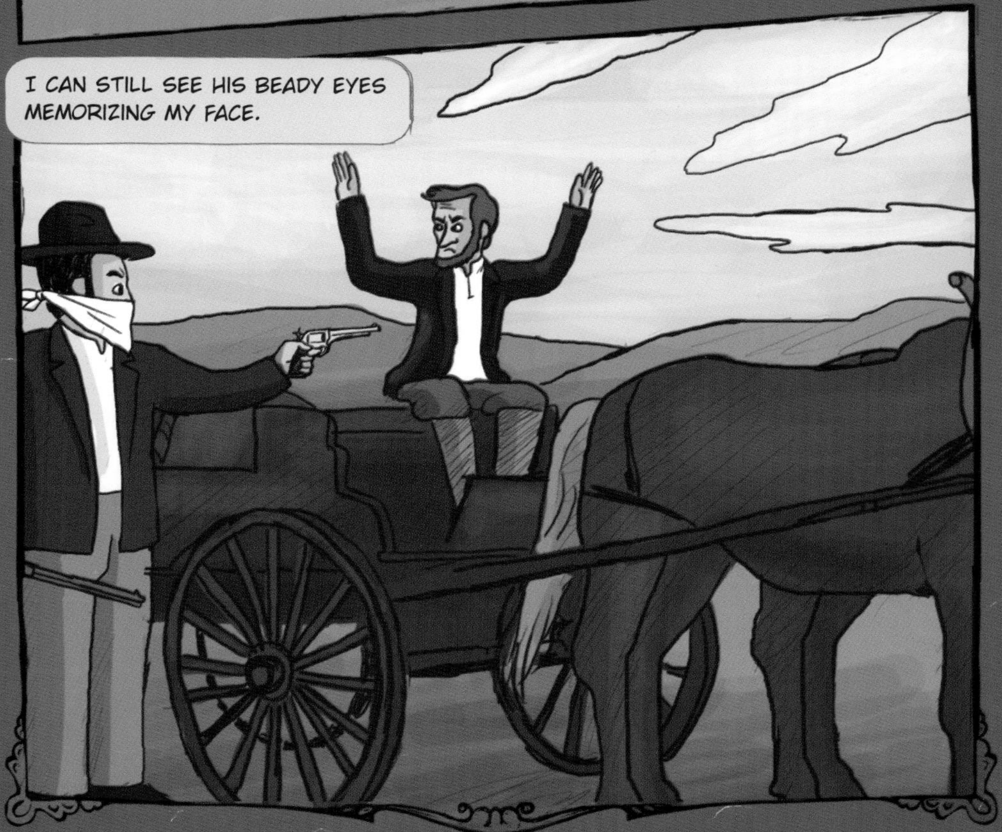
I CAN STILL SEE HIS BEADY EYES MEMORIZING MY FACE.

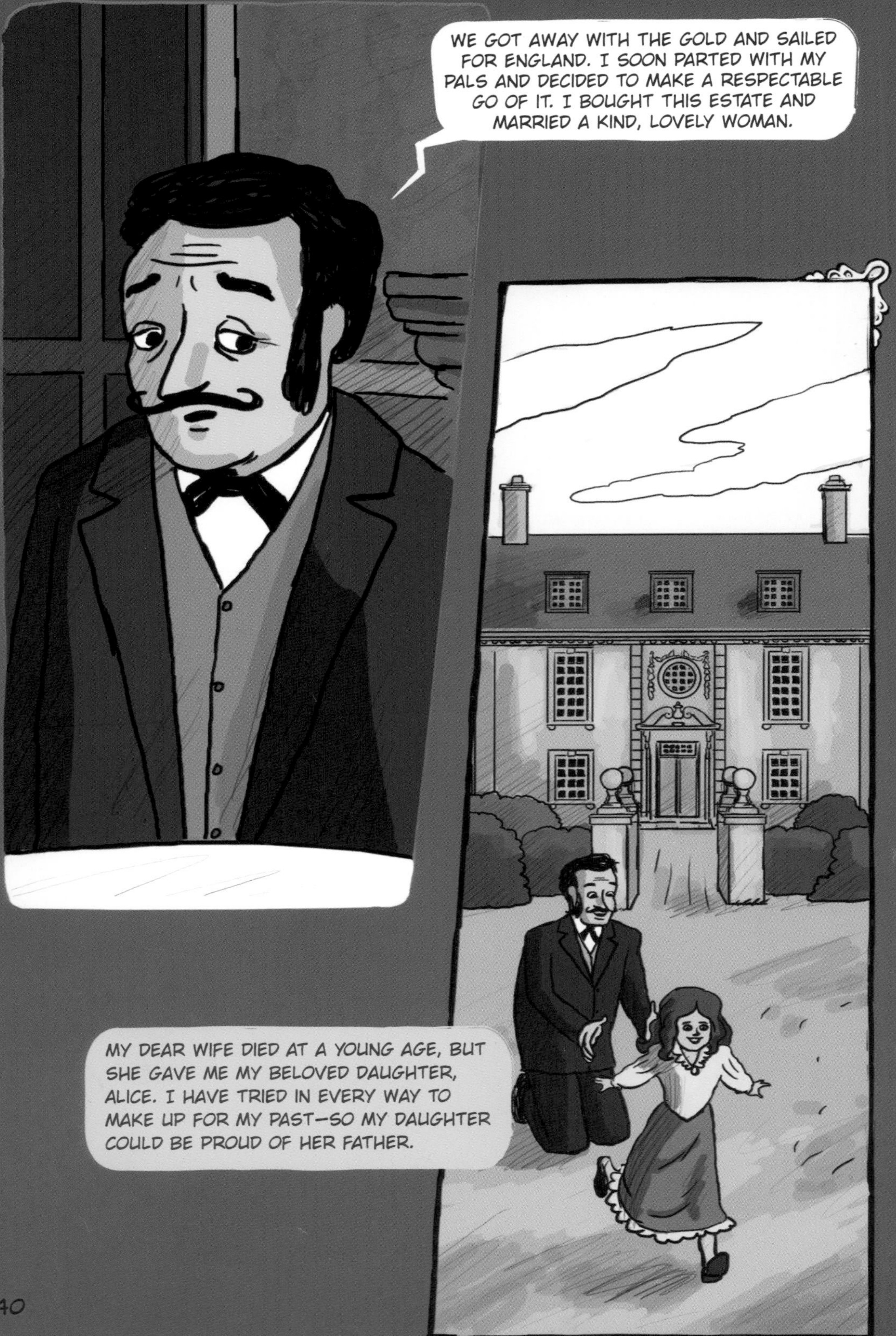
WE GOT AWAY WITH THE GOLD AND SAILED FOR ENGLAND. I SOON PARTED WITH MY PALS AND DECIDED TO MAKE A RESPECTABLE GO OF IT. I BOUGHT THIS ESTATE AND MARRIED A KIND, LOVELY WOMAN.
MY DEAR WIFE DIED AT A YOUNG AGE, BUT SHE GAVE ME MY BELOVED DAUGHTER, ALICE. I HAVE TRIED IN EVERY WAY TO MAKE UP FOR MY PAST—SO MY DAUGHTER COULD BE PROUD OF HER FATHER.

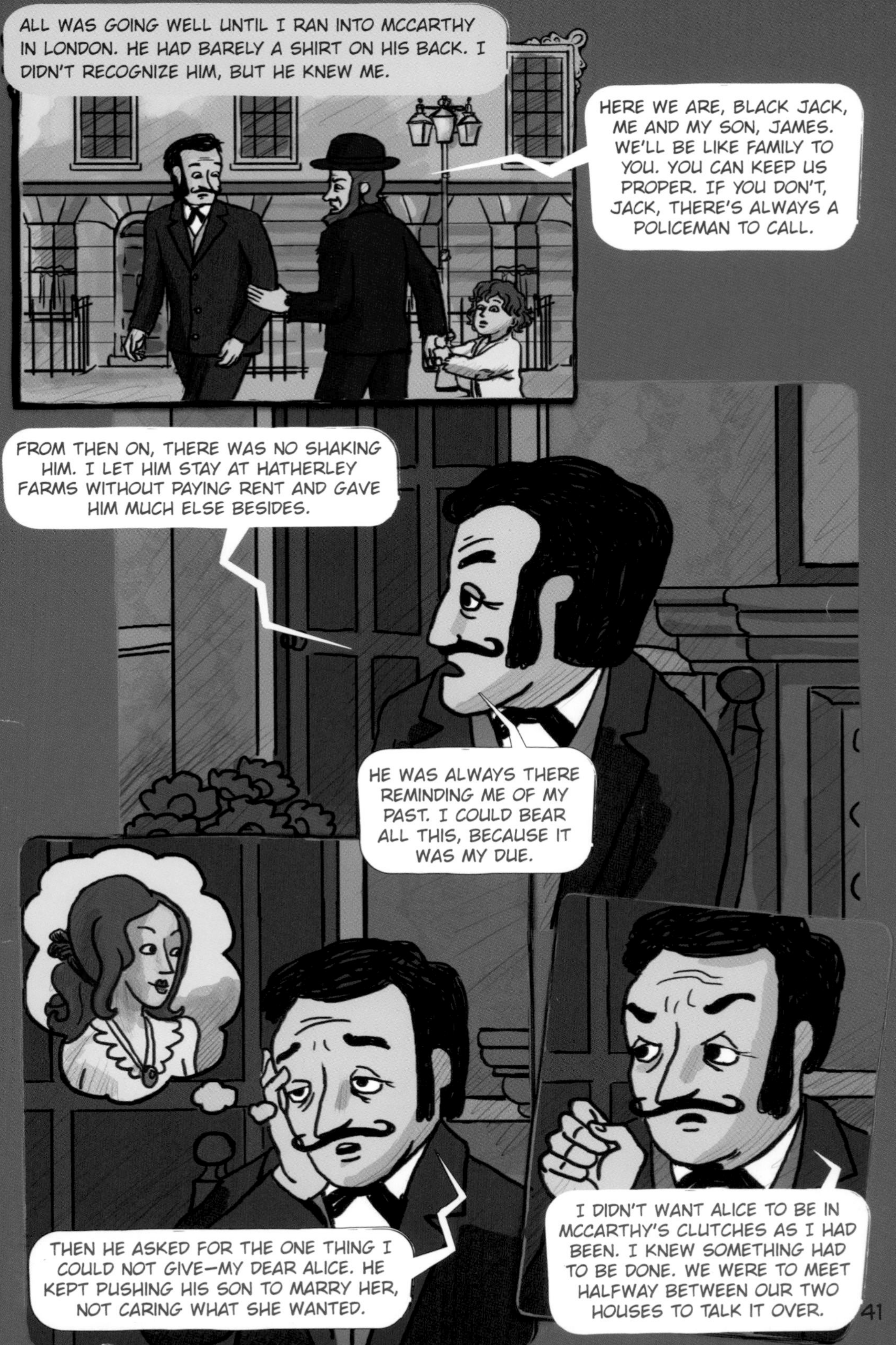
ALL WAS GOING WELL UNTIL I RAN INTO MCCARTHY IN LONDON. HE HAD BARELY A SHIRT ON HIS BACK. I DIDN'T RECOGNIZE HIM, BUT HE KNEW ME.
HERE WE ARE, BLACK JACK, ME AND MY SON, JAMES. WE'LL BE LIKE FAMILY TO YOU. YOU CAN KEEP US PROPER. IF YOU DON'T, JACK, THERE'S ALWAYS A POLICEMAN TO CALL.
FROM THEN ON, THERE WAS NO SHAKING HIM. I LET HIM STAY AT HATHERLEY FARMS WITHOUT PAYING RENT AND GAVE HIM MUCH ELSE BESIDES.
HE WAS ALWAYS THERE REMINDING ME OF MY PAST. I COULD BEAR ALL THIS, BECAUSE IT WAS MY DUE.
THEN HE ASKED FOR THE ONE THING I COULD NOT GIVE—MY DEAR ALICE. HE KEPT PUSHING HIS SON TO MARRY HER, NOT CARING WHAT SHE WANTED.
I DIDN'T WANT ALICE TO BE IN MCCARTHY'S CLUTCHES AS I HAD BEEN. I KNEW SOMETHING HAD TO BE DONE. WE WERE TO MEET HALFWAY BETWEEN OUR TWO HOUSES TO TALK IT OVER.

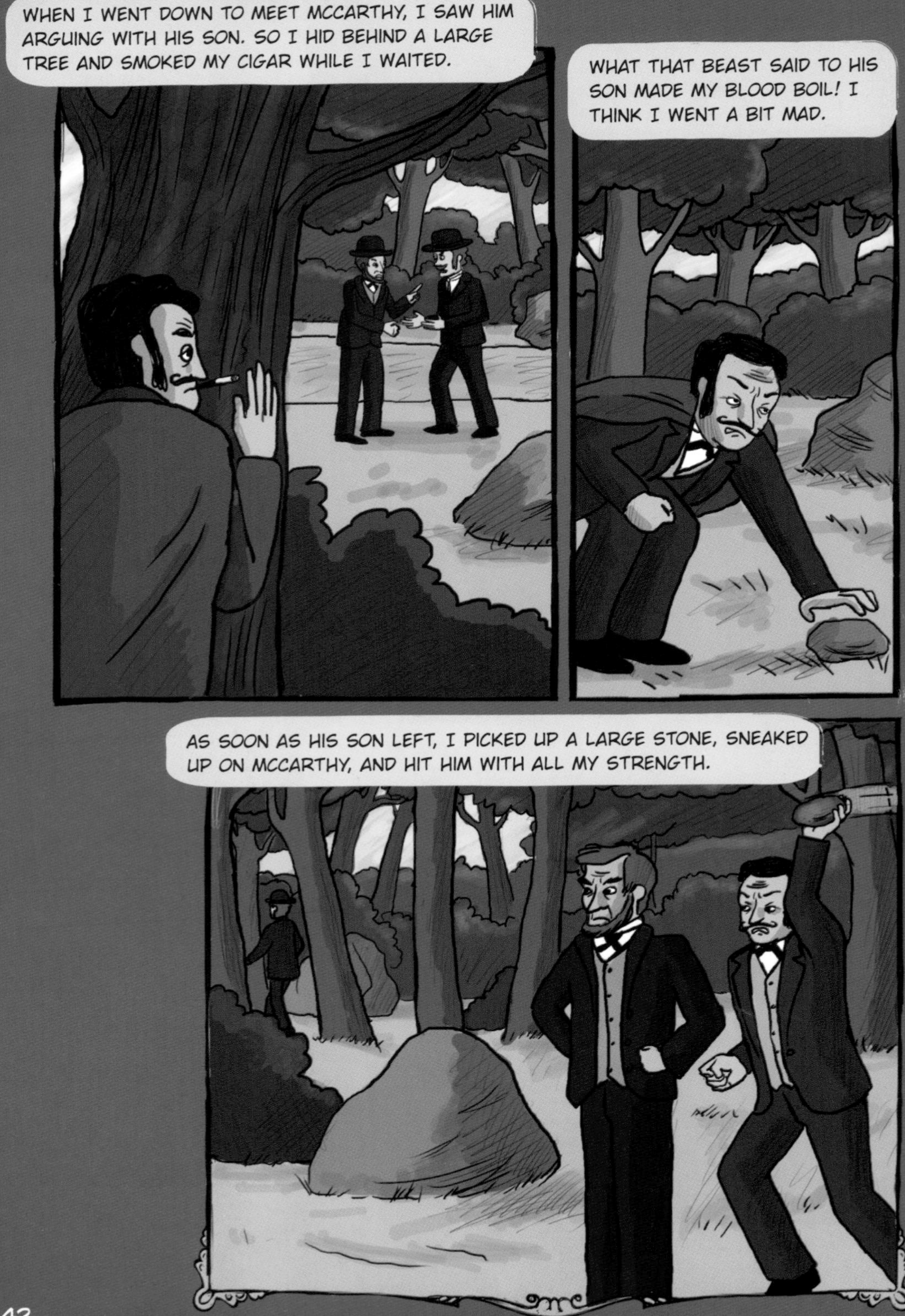
WHEN I WENT DOWN TO MEET MCCARTHY, I SAW HIM ARGUING WITH HIS SON. SO I HID BEHIND A LARGE TREE AND SMOKED MY CIGAR WHILE I WAITED.
WHAT THAT BEAST SAID TO HIS SON MADE MY BLOOD BOIL! I THINK I WENT A BIT MAD.
AS SOON AS HIS SON LEFT, I PICKED UP A LARGE STONE, SNEAKED UP ON MCCARTHY, AND HIT HIM WITH ALL MY STRENGTH.

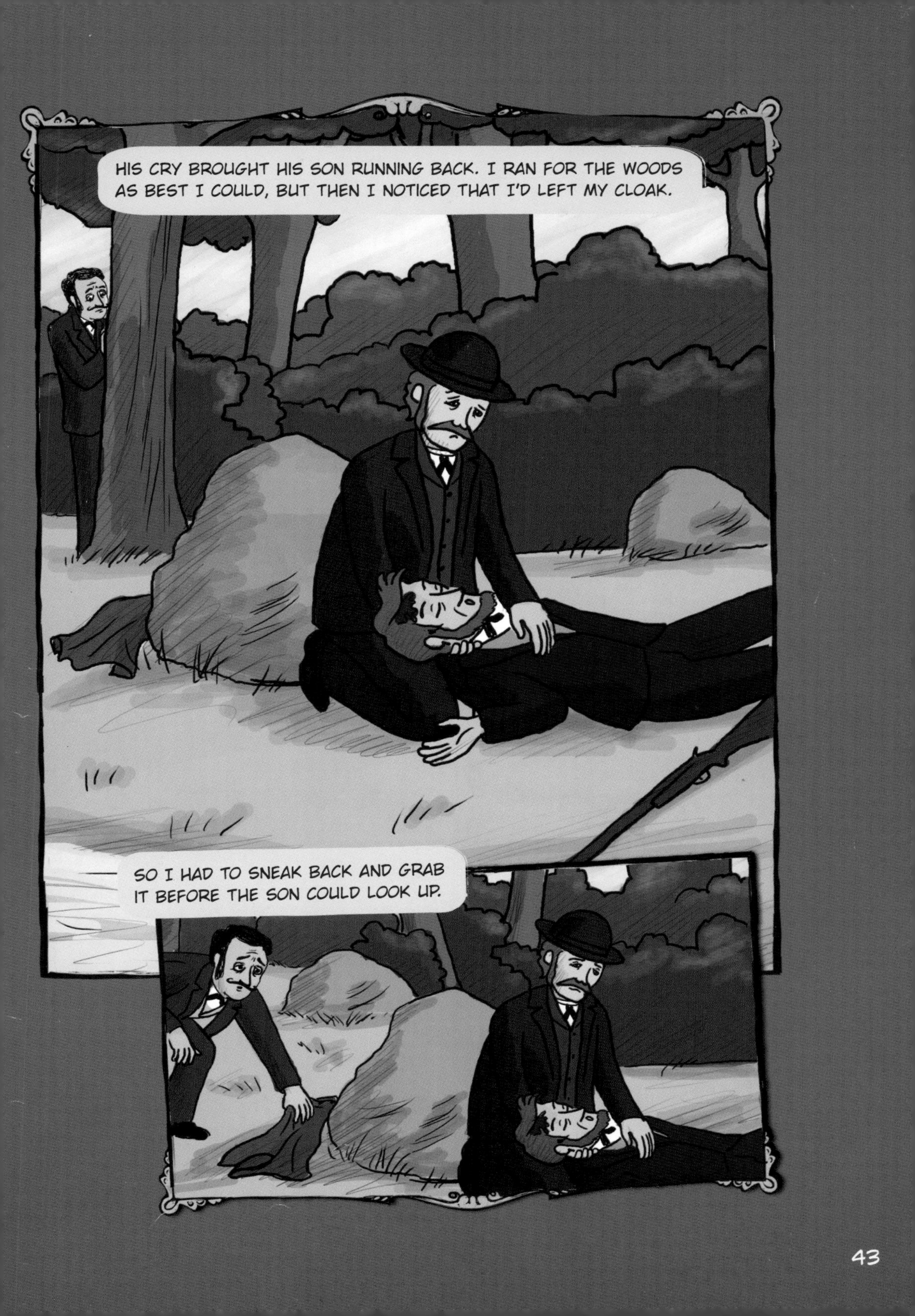
HIS CRY BROUGHT HIS SON RUNNING BACK. I RAN FOR THE WOODS AS BEST I COULD, BUT THEN I NOTICED THAT I'D LEFT MY CLOAK.
SO I HAD TO SNEAK BACK AND GRAB IT BEFORE THE SON COULD LOOK UP.

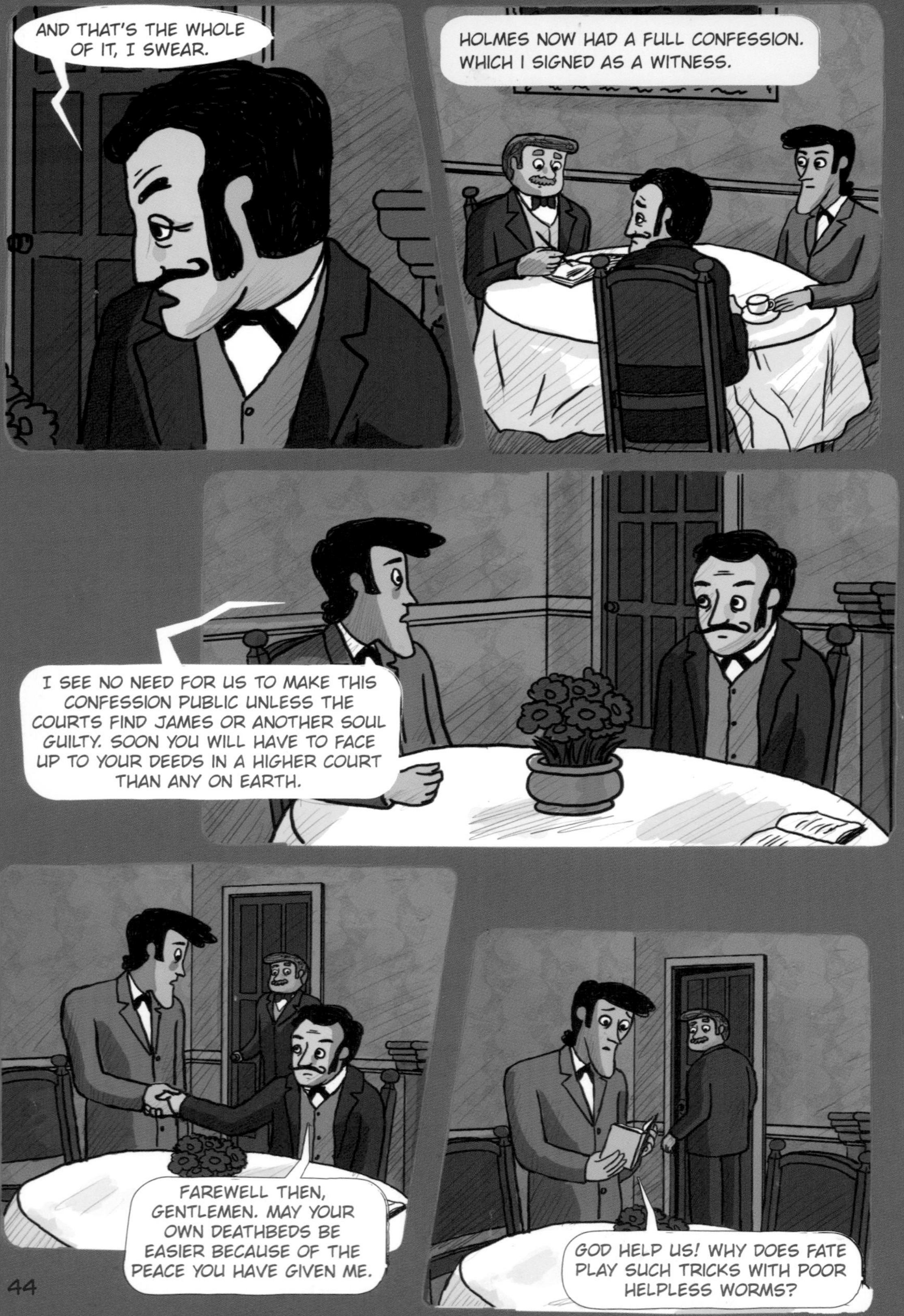
AND THAT'S THE WHOLE OF IT, I SWEAR.
HOLMES NOW HAD A FULL CONFESSION. WHICH I SIGNED AS A WITNESS.
I SEE NO NEED FOR US TO MAKE THIS CONFESSION PUBLIC UNLESS THE COURTS FIND JAMES OR ANOTHER SOUL GUILTY. SOON YOU WILL HAVE TO FACE UP TO YOUR DEEDS IN A HIGHER COURT THAN ANY ON EARTH.
FAREWELL THEN, GENTLEMEN. MAY YOUR OWN DEATHBEDS BE EASIER BECAUSE OF THE PEACE YOU HAVE GIVEN ME.
GOD HELP US! WHY DOES FATE PLAY SUCH TRICKS WITH POOR HELPLESS WORMS?

Old John Turner lived only a few months after we spoke to him. Because of objections raised by Holmes, the courts found James McCarthy to be innocent. No one else was ever accused of the murder. We have heard recently that young McCarthy may soon wed Alice Turner. It is hoped that they will live quite happily. May they never know the black cloud that rests upon their past.

From the Desk of
John H. Watson, M.D.

The Boscombe Valley Mystery: How Did Holmes Solve It?

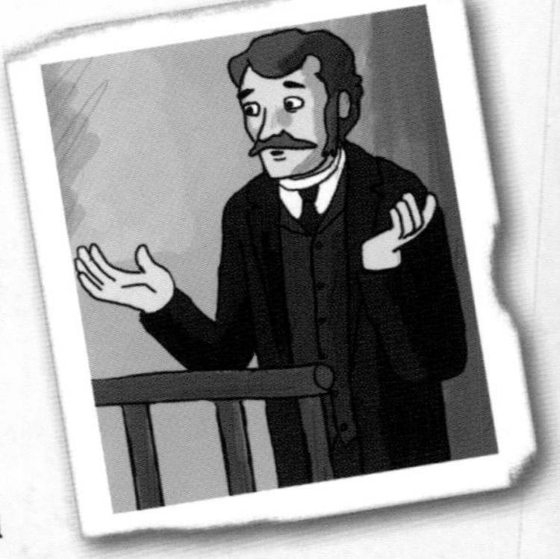

How did Holmes deduce that there was more than one suspect?
Since Charles McCarthy had gone to the Boscombe Pool to meet someone, there were automatically two suspects for the murder: James McCarthy and the person McCarthy had gone to meet. The gamekeeper, Mr. Crowder, also was a suspect, since he had been nearby at the time of the murder.

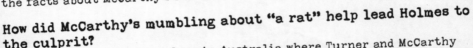

What clue initially led Holmes to consider Turner as a suspect?
According to James McCarthy, his father had called out the Australian greeting "cooee." Since this signal was not meant for James, Charles could have been waiting to meet someone else from Australia. Therefore, Holmes paid close attention to all the facts about McCarthy's Australian friend—John Turner.

How did McCarthy's mumbling about "a rat" help lead Holmes to the culprit?
The maid told Holmes the place in Australia where Turner and McCarthy had met was called Ballarat. The ending could sound like "a rat." The maid had not heard of any recent letters or visits to Mr. McCarthy from Australians. So, Turner immediately became the prime suspect.

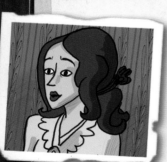

What other clue led Holmes to consider Turner as a suspect?
Holmes also figured there must be some bad feelings between John Turner and Charles McCarthy, since Turner did not want his daughter to marry McCarthy's son. This was another strike against Turner.

How did Holmes's examination of the murder scene lead him to Turner?
By the long lengths between the square-toed footprints, Holmes could see that the murderer was a tall man. The footprints also showed that the man leaned heavily on one foot, so Holmes knew that he limped. The fact that McCarthy had been hit on the left side of his head from behind made it likely that the murderer was left-handed. And finally, by studying the ashes and cigar left at the scene, Holmes could even describe the criminal's smoking habits. All that was left was to find the man who fit this description.

How could Holmes be so certain that he had the right man?
Holmes sent Turner a message, and the man came. Turner fit all the details of the murderer's description. Holmes had no doubt that he had found the right man.

Further Reading and Websites

Baker Street Journal
http://www.bakerstreetjournal.com

Banting, Erinn. *Australia: The People*. New York: Crabtree, 2003.

Carey, Benedict. *The Unknowns*. New York: Amulet Books, 2009.

Dowd, Siobhan. *The London Eye Mystery*. New York: Random House, 2009.

Gregory, Kristiana. *The Clue at the Bottom of the Lake*. New York: Scholastic, 2008.

Marsh, Carole. *The Mystery of the Great Barrier Reef: Sydney, Australia*. New York: Gallopade International, 2006.

McCollum, Sean. *Australia*. Minneapolis: Lerner Publications Company, 2008.

Sherlock Holmes Museum
http://www.sherlock-holmes.co.uk

Sir Arthur Conan Doyle Society
http://www.ash-tree.bc.ca/acdsocy.html

Townsend, John. *Forensic Evidence: Prints*. New York: Crabtree Publishing, 2008.

221 Baker Street
http://221bakerstreet.org

About the Author

Sir Arthur Conan Doyle was born on May 22, 1859. He became a doctor in 1882. When this career did not prove successful, Doyle started writing stories. In addition to the popular Sherlock Holmes short stories and novels, Doyle also wrote historical novels, romances, and plays.

About the Adapters

Murray Shaw's lifelong passion for Sherlock Holmes began when he was a child. He was the author of the Match Wits with Sherlock Holmes series published in the 1990s. For decades, he was a popular speaker in public schools and libraries on the adventures of Holmes and Watson.

M. J. Cosson is the author of more than fifty books, both fiction and nonfiction, for children and young adults. She has long been a fan of mysteries and especially of the great detective, Sherlock Holmes. In fact, she has participated in the production of several Sherlock Holmes plays. A native of Iowa, Cosson lives in the Texas Hill Country with her husband, dogs, and cat.

About the Illustrators

Sophie Rohrbach began her career after graduating in display design at the Chambre des Commerce in France. She went on to design displays in many top department stores including Galerias Lafayette. She also studied illustration at Emile Cohl school in Lyon, France, where she now lives with her daughter. Rohrbach has illustrated many children's books. She is passionate about the colors and patterns that she uses in her illustrations.

JT Morrow has worked as a freelance illustrator for over twenty years and has won several awards. He specializes in doing parodies and imitations of the Old and Modern Masters—everyone from da Vinci to Picasso. JT also exhibits his paintings at galleries near his home. He lives just south of San Francisco with his wife and daughter.